LIV & CALLUM

Miley German

CONTENTS

Un Happy Hour (Olivia) — 1

Can I Call You?(Olivia) — 13

11 PM (Olivia) — 18

Last Halloween (Callum) — 29

Natural History (Callum) — 35

Thanks for Dinner (Callum) — 47

Chapter 7: Liv — 56

Chapter 8: Callum — 65

Chapter 9: Liv — 71

Chapter 10: Callum — 77

Chapter 11: Liv — 86

Chapter 12: Callum — 91

Chapter 13 — 105

un Happy Hour (Olivia)

There's something about stepping away from the kids during the day that makes me feel like I'm playing hooky. I'm checking my phone constantly and rushing to get home so that I don't run into anyone. I can practically see the flashing neon sign above me that says, "absentee mother".

In reality, the kids are with their aunt and I am meeting a friend for coffee, but that doesn't lessen the elicit feeling of driving in my car without a tinny little voice in the backseat asking me for a snack pouch.

I check my phone again when I arrive at the cafe that Jamie and I like. Andrea, my sister, has sent me 11 pictures of my three year old daughter, Annie, in her cousin's dinosaur costume from last year. Based on past behavior, I'm assuming that'll be coming home with

Annie and it's all she'll wear for the next week. I find myself smiling at the idea of making her dino shaped nuggets to eat while she wears her new favorite outfit.

God, I love being a mom but I am also incredibly grateful for my sister, mother, and friends who allow me to take time away from that job. I send back a heart emoji and ask Andrea if she wants me to bring her a coffee when I pick up Annie.

The sun is intense when I get out of the car, and I'm glad that I snagged a spot in the shade. Pulling open the door, Jamie's head turns towards me at the sound of the bell above the door. She's managed to get our favorite table at this cafe; it's a bench seat under a bay window and it's like I'm finally in my dream beach cottage. I might not be close to living in my little cottage, but the cushy bench seat and a good friend is a lovely placeholder.

"Hi Liv!"

"Hello gorgeous. I'm going to grab my coffee and then I'll head back to our seats. Need anything?"

"No thanks, I got here a little early so I had a chance to order already. See you in a sec."

With that, I head to the front counter and choose from their new seasonal lattes. An iced blueberry latte seems like the perfect answer to a sunny day.

While I'm waiting in line, I send the cutest of the pictures of our Annie-saurus Rex to Callum. Surprisingly, I get an immediate read receipt and he gives a thumbs up to one of the pictures. He must have had his phone out already because usually I will have to ask him about a text when he comes home in the evening, since he's so bad about responding during the day.

To be fair, I know that his team has been working on a proposal for a company called CXE that would elevate the clientele at the firm where he and Jamie both work. Lately it's all he can focus on, but I know that these things come and go and it's the nature of being married to a man as intense and driven as Callum. All the same, I'll be glad when he's finished with this pitch and he has more time to spend with me and Annie. In the last few weeks he's only been home 10 or 20 minutes before she goes to bed and I know that she feels his absence as well.

"What did you end up trying?" Jamie knows that I can't resist the shiny new marketing for a new flavor.

"This time I went with a blueberry latte," I take a moment to grab a cautious sip, "and it is miles better than the cranberry flavor that they tried last month."

"Well for $6 I would certainly hope so."

"Hey! Not everyone developed a fancy palette while they were living abroad in college." I draw out 'abroad' and put on a fanciful accent to give her a little ribbing. When she first came back from her European semester she fell into every stereotype of the American who studied abroad. 7 years later and I still like to remind her occasionally.

"That's very true, most people could never touch my superior and expert taste for folgers and cold espresso shots that I forget about."

"Very true. I appreciate that you'll even consider being seen in public near a fruit flavored latte." I throw a wink her way over the rim of my coffee cup on my next sip.

"I take a second to look at one of my oldest friends, and I can't help but notice that she looks a bit...unsettled.

Her black pumps are swinging under our seats with the motion of her jittery leg, long fingers are gripping her porcelain espresso cup too tightly, and her shoulders seem more tense than usual. Jamie is, by nature, a high strung woman but this feels different.

"Is everything okay?" We've never spent too much time beating around the bush.

Her shoulders sink a bit, but the gesture is more defeated and relaxed.

"Honestly, not really and I'm trying to figure out how to approach this." She's still not really looking at me.

"Is it something at work? I know that Cal has been stressing about this project for CXE."

Usually, Callum and Jamie work on a small team to build their proposals but that nature of this bud means that they had to bring on other consultants, architects, and engineers.

"Kind of, actually." There's a few beats while I watch her decide how she wants to vent. "Do you remember the architect that I was telling you about?"

"Only vaguely, just that you mentioned her in passing"

"Okay, well her name is Emily and I've been noticing a few things that I want to run by you, and maybe just...I don't know, make sure that you're aware of?" She phrases it like a question, which undercuts how uncomfortable Jamie is with this conversation.

I furrow my brows and then nod my head for her to keep going.

"Okay. I don't know if I'm being sensitive because I love you so much, or if I'm reading into things but I feel icky not talking to you about it. A few weeks ago we were at a luncheon and she referred to Cal as her "work husband" when we were talking about the hours that we've had to put in lately. Since then it's become sort of a running joke between Cal and Emily, and he'll refer to her as his "work wife" to other people." Jamie starts leaning forward and suddenly I realize that she is now making intense eye contact with me, and she's put her coffee down.

"Hmmm." A sip of my latte gives me a moment to think. "I'll admit that I don't love the idea of my husband referring to anyone as his wife, even as a joke, but that might just be an awkward office joke."

"That's the thing though, no one else really makes the joke. If it were everyone or if someone said it first I would just assume that they're going along with a bit, but no one else talks about it. They'll say something like, 'Oh, got to ask my work wife before I say yes' or 'I don't know, I'll have to see if the work hubby agrees' even when they aren't around each other."

"Jamie, are you trying to tell me that Callum might cheat on me?" I don't see any way around the question.

"I have absolutely no evidence and I really don't want to cause issues or overstep. I don't think that they're having an affair or anything, but it has just been making me feel weird and I don't want to feel like I'm hiding something from you when I see you."

If Jamie feels like I need to know, then I can't brush it off. She has better intuition than most and I have to believe that She would have thought long and hard about speaking to me before she did. She and Callum have a friendship separate from me, and she knows him better than most.

"Is there anything else that you've noticed? I think that I need to talk to him about this tonight and I need a full picture."

"When she first came on to this pitch I thought that it seemed like she had a thing for Cal. Obviously you and Cal both get hit on plenty, and I do think that flirting can be harmless, but they've been having more closed door meetings and lunches this week. I asked him once if he needed any other team members in on their meetings and he said that they were just work sessions and she had ideas that she wanted to run past him before bringing to the team. I'm serious when I say that I don't think they're having an affair, but I do think that there is something weird there and you deserve to know."

"How do I talk to Cal about it? I feel like it would be weird to tell him that I've heard about a weird joke that he may or may not have with a coworker or that I'm not comfortable with him taking meetings with her."

"First off, the way that you feel is important in any contact. He deserves to know that something he's doing is making you uncomfortable and you deserve a relationship where your partner can talk things through with you. Isn't that what you all normally do?"

Jamie is right, naturally. Cal and I have always talked about how we're feeling in our relationship, and especially in the beginning we both had to make changes to have a healthy relationship together.

"You're right. And normally I wouldn't feel weird about mentioning it but I just feel like I rarely see him anymore. Between Annie, me just starting work again, and his schedule I think that we're in the roommate stage. He doesn't come home until late and then we're doing bedtime with a toddler, I'm trying to get caught up on house stuff, one of us is working out, and it just goes on and on. We're not particularly connected right now and I'm just not feeling very-" I pause abruptly here. Saying it out loud makes me realize how disconnected I currently feel from Cal.

We've always been on the more passionate and attached side of things, but I don't remember the last time that we were intimate, physically or emotionally.

Jamie lets me decompress for a moment, but gently presses on. "I get that, and I've heard that these stages happen in long term relationships, especially after kids. It's normal to feel that way. Heck, you and

I have felt that way about our relationship and we've just been honest about it and planned more friend-dates. Do you and Cal have any upcoming opportunities to take some time together? Even just for a few hours."

"I don't see how, other than asking him to not work while he's home. He's been so honed in on this project that I don't even know if he would say yes. And then the idea of bringing the work wife up with him just makes me really anxious that he's going to get stressed out even more about work. It's not that I think he would be mad, because I know that he'd talk it out with me, but then I'm just adding to his plate. Maybe I just buckle down until this is over and then tell him that I'd prefer that he try to prioritize his work/life balance better in the future. That's the real issue, and I haven't even seen him and Emily together enough to know if it's a real issue."

"Then why don't you come to the happy hour tonight? I know that Andrea can't keep Annie tonight but I can pick her up and have a fun auntie evening. I also haven't seen enough of Annie and if I don't hang out with her on a regular basis I might get the crazy idea that I'm ready for kids."

We both smile at that because Jamie and Annie are the best of friends, but being around Annie does seem to satisfy Jamie's maternal instincts and remind her that she likes a quiet and clean home. Then something she said makes me sit up a little straighter.

"Wait, what do you mean Andrea can't keep Annie tonight?"

Jamie's mouth thins into a frown. "Cal said that you didn't want to leave Annie with a sitter and Andrea couldn't keep her tonight, which is why you said no to the happy hour tonight."

"He never asked me about a happy hour. All I knew about tonight is that Cal has a work thing that's going to keep him later than usual. Annie is with Andrea right now, and I haven't even asked her if she can keep her later. Did Cal tell you that I wasn't coming?" It's getting hot in here, and the sun coming from the window is suddenly too bright, too harsh.

"Shit, Liv, he told me today that's why you weren't coming tonight."

Jamie is holding my left hand now, and my right is clutching my forgotten latte, wet with the perspiration on the cup. I look over and see that the ice has melted so much that there's a thin layer of water sitting untouched over the milky coffee below. What a waste of $6.00. I wonder if they would add more ice and remix it for me.

"Liv?"

"Hmm?" Maybe an extra espresso shot? Although there's no way I'd ask them to do that for free.

"Are you okay? Do you want to table this conversation and wait until you've talked to Cal?"

Right. Yes. Callum. A happy hour that, apparently, I declined an invitation to.

"I'm not actually really sure what I'm feeling right now. I used to come to these things with you guys all the time and now I can't remember the last time I went. Do you all still do them every month or so?"

I used to love the little themed happy hour and parties at Jamie and Callum's office. I would get to dress up a bit and meet people, and Cal used to tell me that he thought his boss just kept him around so that he could try to charm me at company functions. Admittedly, his boss is quite the flirt but I also know that he is over the moon in love with his wonderful wife and most of the time we're off in a corner talking about parenting or sharing family photos.

Jamie grimaces and nods her head, confirming that I have been left out of the last month of these gatherings. I haven't always been able to go, because I have Annie and I also freelance, but Cal hasn't even asked.

"I think that I need to think for a bit. Do you mind if I take off? I might take the long way home and figure out how to talk to Cal."

"Of course. Honestly, I probably need to get back because this client really is a handful. I'll be here if you need to talk it through or vent or anything, alright?"

"I know. Thank you for telling me. Truly, from what you've told me I guess we're even more disconnected than I realized and I think that I need to just get it all out there as soon as possible."

We bus our table, wave goodbye to the barista behind the counter, and hug in the parking lot before going our separate ways to our cars. I sit behind the wheel for a second, waiting for the a/c to cool down the muggy interior.

Well fuck. This sucks.

I can feel the unease in my body build up through my stomach and into my throat. I have always been the kind of person who feels emotions very physically, especially when I'm anxious about something. I can't stand this feeling and if I've learned anything in therapy it's that I need to confront my emotions instead of putting them off.

I pull out my phone and go to my text thread with Cal.

Me: Can I call you?

Can I Call You? (Olivia)

Me: Can I call you?

Cal: Everything okay?

Me: It's not an emergency but I do really need to talk to you.

Cal: Can it wait until tomorrow?

Why do I feel like I'm pulling teeth?

Me: Not really. Do you have 5-10 minutes?

Cal: Why can't we just text? It's easier for me while I'm at work.

Me: I just need to talk to you.

Cal: Fine, give me two minutes to ask my colleagues to excuse me and then I'll call you when I'm out.

It takes him 7 minutes.

"Hey, what's going on?"

"They really didn't want to let you go, did they?"

"Huh? Liv, is everything okay?"

"I just meant that it took you a while to call, they must have not wanted to let you go."

"Yeah, it took a second. You know this pitch has been intense and I had to explain why I was stepping out of our brainstorming session." His tone is tight and rushed, and I can't hear my partner in the words that he's saying or the way that he's talking to me.

"Who's in your brainstorming session?"

"Jesus, Liv, one of the other consultants that you haven't met. What's going on? What did you need to talk about in the middle of the day?"

"I wish that I could meet her tonight, at the happy hour. It sucks that Andrea can't keep Annie tonight which means that I can't go."

Cal lets out a whoosh of air on the other line, but I don't pause too long.

"Did you lie to your coworkers and tell them that I couldn't come tonight?"

"Olivia-I." But he doesn't finish his sentence. The pause is so long that, if I couldn't hear his breath, I wouldn't know that he was still on the line.

"It feels like you lied, Callum. Do you not want me to be there?"

"It's not that I don't want you to be there, I just know that Annie wears you out during the day and you've been trying to get more contracts signed so that you can rebuild your clientele independently. I didn't want you to feel obligated to come to my things as well."

That car is finally cool enough, but maybe I left that a/c on too high because my fingers feel stiff around my steering wheel. I take a moment to turn the a/c down but I don't feel any rush of warmth.

"I wish that you would have asked me, Cal. It put Jaime in an uncomfortable position when she realized that I didn't know about it, and it made me feel really small when I had to admit that you didn't even ask me. Have I made it seem as if I feel obliged to go in the past?"

"I just know how busy you've been with trying to get clients and-," I'm rude, and I interrupt him here.

"I already have contracts signed and I've had the same work schedule for the last few weeks. I told you that last week."

"Well I'm sorry that I forgot what you told me." Why does he sound annoyed with me? I don't know how to respond to that bullshit apology.

"So are you coming tonight?" Is he kidding?

"No. I am not coming and I would appreciate it if you would only stay for a little while. I really want to talk this out, Cal. My feelings are hurt and Andrea can keep Annie for the night so that we can get this figured out."

"Why can't you just stay up a little later when I get home? WHy do I have to come home early? It's important for me to network and we have to do teambuilding to make it work with all of the new people we hired for this pitch. These things are important for me, Liv."

"Cal, the new people have been on your team for 6 weeks already and I don't see how you're going to do any new networking with Josh from Change Management who has been there for 6 years."

"Well that's because you don't have to get it! But I'm expected to be at these things, even if you don't tag along. You always go to bed super early, why can't you just stay up for an extra 20 minutes so that we can talk."

"I can compromise and stay up a little later but I would also like you to come home earlier. You said that you wouldn't be home until 9:30 or 10 and I still have to get up with Annie tomorrow."

"Fine, what if I got home at 9?"

"Sure."

"Okay."

What do you even say after a conversation like this ?

"I have to go, I'm being waved back in. The picture of Annie was cute, thanks for sending it." As olive branches go, it was anemic and stilted.

"9?"

"Yeah, I'll see you at 9."

11 PM (Olivia)

I don't see him at 9.

I don't see him at 9:30.

I don't see him at 10:00.

It's 10:15 when I put away the wine glasses that I put out on the coffee table. It's 10:20 when I do my final sweep of the house and check in with Andrea to make sure that Annie settled. She loves her auntie and cousins, so of course she did. We make plans for me to get her in the morning.

It's 10:45 when I hear Cal's key in the door, the deadbolt sliding back into place. I can hear him try to avoid the creaky spots in our old floorboards, but they're all creaky. He waits until he's in our adjoining bathroom to turn the light on and start his shower. It doesn't really matter, because I can't bring myself to admit that I stayed up even later for him.

It's 11:00 when he slips into bed and I realize that my marriage, my partnership, is in a much worse state than the roommate stage.

If there's one thing that I can count on, it's that my alarm will go off at 5:15. Cal can sleep through almost anything, so It's never been a huge issue that I'm an early riser and he's a night owl. This morning, however, I don't take the extra care that I usually do to be quiet while he sleeps.

I roll out of bed and let my pillow flop behind me. I turn the light on in the bathroom before I close the door, and I close the door harder than I usually would. I'm being passive aggressive, which I usually hate, but I'm feeling raw and neglected and if Cal wanted more sleep then he should have been home earlier.

The hot shower doesn't do much for me this morning, and it's because I can still feel a balloon of anxiety in my diaphragm. Even though I love Cal, and I know that he loves me, there is a bone-deep uneasiness that I feel this morning. Something slimy and foreboding that sticks inside.

The sound of the bathroom door opening and then snicking shut breaks me out of my trance, and I stop staring at the wall. I know Cal woke up, probably because of me, but I did most of the talking yesterday and I feel like it's his turn. Instead, I turn to our shower caddy and pick up my favorite overpriced shampoo.

"Can I join you?" I move the shower curtain to peek at Cal, and I probably shouldn't have. The dark green of the curtain gives the hot shower a feel of safety that rushes out and is replaced by cold air. Now I'm chilly, but I take a second to look at my husband.

He has always been gorgeous, to me and most other people. Teetering between 5'11" and 6', Cal keeps in shape and has an olive tone to his skin that gives him a year round tan. He doesn't have a 6-pack, but regular visits to the gym and a healthy diet have kept him muscular, with a little belly that shows he still enjoys ice cream with his daughter and a few glasses of whiskey every week. His hair is dark and thick, and compliments the beard that he brushes and oils every day.

When we were dating, he kept it stubbly but I kept getting rashes so he grew it out and it's done wonders for him. A sharp jaw, strong dimpled chin, and wide shoulders round out a truly delicious package.

If we were having this conversation yesterday, I would have relished the opportunity to let him wash my hair, which has always been a particular favorite ritual between us. I don't remember the last time I felt his hands on my scalp, though, and that adds a bitter sadness to the anxiety I'm feeling.

"No thanks, I'm almost done." Even to my own ears my voice sounds too nonchalant.

I'm working conditioner into the ends of my hair when he tries again, probably not expecting my rejection after the way that I've been clinging to him when he's home these last few weeks.

"I'm sorry that I was short with you on the phone yesterday, and I'm sorry that I came home late after promising that I would be home at 9. It was shitty of me to do that, and I don't like how I treated you yesterday."

That's a start, maybe.

"I also don't like how you treated me yesterday. Thank you for apologizing for coming home late, but I think that we have larger issues that need to be resolved. I've been dancing around this for a while because I understand that you've been busy and stressed with work, but I feel like Annie and I barely get to see you. When you are home, it feels like your mind is somewhere else and she and I are both struggling."

"Can we finish this conversation when you're out of the shower? I don't like having this kind of conversation when I can't look at you."

Luckily for him, I finished washing my face and rinsing my hair when he was talking. I lean over to shut off the water and give myself one more desperate moment in my warm shower cocoon, but all things must end.

I pull open the shower curtain and Cal is now leaning against the sink, brushing his teeth. Without saying anything, I move to take my toothbrush out of the medicine cabinet at my side of the sink. He hands me the toothpaste and we begin the mundane task of brushing our teeth, me dripping water onto the rug and him taking furtive glances out of the corner of his eye.

Cal and I have had great chemistry, even through pregnancy and postpartum. That's part of why our recent distance has felt so much worse to me. We have always enjoyed the daily ritual of caring for eachother, and building intimacy and connection through a long hug, quick kisses, brushing the other person's hair, or a scratch of the nails down the back. We haven't had that in a while, and it isn't until now that I have to swallow the hard truth that my husband doesn't touch me anymore.

I've been the one reaching out, and maybe I've been overcompensating because I subconsciously realize that he isn't engaging with me anymore. Maybe I'm touching him too much, trying too hard, and pushing him away as a result. As I stare at myself in the mirror and finish brushing my teeth, I suddenly cannot stand being naked around him. I don't want to feel his glances, or risk brushing against him without the barrier of clothes between us.

When I drop my toothbrush back in the medicine cabinet I pivot to our towel rack and wrap myself securely in one of our big waffle knit bath sheets.

"Don't cover up on my behalf?"

I spare him a glance before starting my morning body and face routine. "This isn't funny, Cal, and I don't want to feel this way about you and be naked at the same time."

"Feel what way about me?" He also starts his routine, and I know it as well as my own. Face wash, moisturizer, beard oil and brush, hair pomade, deodorant, cologne. I can list off the steps and I repeat it in my head to help me refocus.

"I am feeling incredibly vulnerable around you right now. I am hurt and disappointed that you came home an hour and 45 minutes after you said that you would be home. I was very clear yesterday that I was upset about you lying to your coworkers about why I wouldn't be at the happy hour, and I wanted to be able to talk about that with you. Now that I have had more time to think, I am realizing how disjointed we have become and how little intimacy we have in our current relationship. I feel like we have a much more serious issue on our hands than a lie about a happy hour."

I'm onto my hair routine as my serums soak in, and I think about what I have on my agenda today. No client meetings, so I can be a bit more casual. I throw in some air dry clean and decide on going with my natural waves today.

"Live, I agree that what I did yesterday was shitty. I came home later than I should, but I don't think that being home at 10 instead of 9 is anything deeper than me losing track of time. I can work on that but I don't want us to tiptoe around each other. Again, I'm sorry for being late and snipping at you on the phone. I also didn't ask you to come because I didn't want you to sacrifice your time to come to a borning work event with your husband's coworkers."

"It's not just about you being late one night or not wanting to burden my feelings. You came home almost two hours late, Callum. I waited on the couch until 10:15 and I was awake when you got home. Two hours is not losing track of time, it's a choice that you made to not be considerate of my feelings. You're an adult, and you have no problem being on time to the things that you care about."

"I-," he's already trying to respond the second that I take a breath.

"Wait a second, I am not done. I need to finish this thought and then I will listen to you." He nods at me through the mirror to keep going.

"It hurts my feelings that you didn't even ask if I wanted to go. I have been taking on the vast majority of childcare for the last few months that you've been chasing after CXE. You haven't had to think about who has Annie or if her needs are being met, because I stepped up to the plate when you told me that you would be busy. Fine, I get that not everything is 50/50 the whole time and I want to support your ambitions. But it's been two months, and in that time you haven't been considering my need to get out of the house without a toddler. I would have loved the chance to get dressed up and talk to people our age but instead of that chance, you decided for me that I was better off spending another night doing dinner, bath time, and night time stories by myself. How is that a break? A break would have been to skip a happy hour and spend one on one time with a daughter who has been missing you every day."

The more that I talk the more that a hot spear of anger deflates the anxiety in my gut. Jesus, I am angry at my husband and I hate how that feels. I move into our bedroom to grab my clothes for the day.

"You're right, and I didn't realize how much I would be taking on with this project. I miss you and Annie all the time, and I think about my family constantly. But this would be a huge step for my career, and I want to be in a good financial position for a second baby, or a vacation, or college funds. This project can give me that. Can you stick this out a little longer? We present in a week and either way it goes I'll have more time to be at home."

I'm dressed in bike shorts and one of my favorite old college shirts by the time Cal moved to our bedroom to choose his suit.

"I didn't call you yesterday to ask about the happy hour, at least not entirely. We got hung up on it and now I have noticed more, but that wasn't what sparked this."

He's looking at me wearily while he secures his cufflinks, but doesn't say anything.

"Who is Emily?"

He ducks his gaze to the tie he's securing, but my heart clenches because he's been wearing a tie since he was 18. He could tie a double Windsor with his eyes closed and doesn't need to watch his hands for a single knot.

"She's an architectural consultant who he hired for this project."

"Do you call her your work wife?"

"Yeah, as a joke. It doesn't mean anything."

"It makes me uncomfortable."

"Where is this coming from, Liv? You've never been jealous of a random coworker before."

"You really think that I'm jealous? Callum, I'm uncomfortable because I feel that you making that joke is disrespectful to our relationship. Furthermore, we have not been in a spot like this before and I feel like our relationship is weaker than it's ever been. If we were doing well and I felt like you were actively engaged with me then, yeah, maybe I wouldn't feel this way. But you aren't and I do. Are you listening to me? Because it feels like you think this is just a snippy little argument about a coworker and a party. This is serious Callum, and I'm not sure that you're listening to me enough to understand the gravity of this conversation.

"Of course I understand that this is serious. I've never seen you act like this before so I get that this is different, but I still feel like this will get worked out when this project is finished and I can be more present with you and Annie. I know that we're not seeing each other very much and I'm not handling this workload as well as I thought I could, but that's temporary. We'll be back to us soon."

"I'm not sure that's true Cal. This feels big."

"Well try to remember that we love each other, and we're in this together. We'll get out on the other side."

We both walk downstairs in silence. He seems settled, as if we worked it out and we agreed that this is just an isolated rough patch. I'm quiet because I don't know what good it would do to talk to him. It's like he's not seeing me, and I don't know how else to reach him. I tell him that I am feeling vulnerable and that our relationship is the weakest it's ever been, and he tells me that we need to stick it out for the sake of his career?

I agree with him that we'll get to the "other side" of this, but I'm becoming less and less certain that the other side will look anything like the life I thought that we were building.

A/N: We have Callum's POV next!

Last Halloween (Callum)

Callum

I hate arguing with Liv. As a rule, we don't and I think that's why I feel a vague sort of itchiness as I watch her leave to go pick up Olivia. Seeing her come out of the shower this morning made me realize how long it's been since we had enough alone time to just be two people who love each other.

Despite my jumpiness, I still watch her round ass and shapely legs as she walks out of the door. She looks a little more muscular than she did a few weeks ago, and I wonder if she's been working out more. Between being a supermom to Annie and trying to pull in more clients for her freelance data analyst business, I'm not sure how she would find the time.

That reminds me of a thought I had during our snit this morning, and I pulled out my phone to make a call. I take an extra moment to look my my screensaver; it's a photo that I took of Liv and Annie last Halloween. Annie went as a ladybug and made Liv dress up like a bumblebee because of a movie we had watched about animated bugs. Liv was holding Annie and making goofy buzzing noises and Annie was just about losing her little baby mind about how funny her mom is. I was walking behind them at the perfect moment to capture a truly beautiful interaction between mother and daughter.

I wasn't lying to Liv when I told her that I miss my family all the time, but I'm also thinking of the little beach cottage that Liv wants, hopefully welcoming a sibling for Annie, and sending however many children we have to school or helping them get a good start in life. I can support them better if I can prove the the firm partners that I have what it takes to pull in a client like CXE. I might be looking at my own partner position and I can't ignore something like that. We'll get through this, and I'll put in for PTO today so that I can surprise my girls with a trip away or something.

I made a mental note to email my boss about some time off after our CXE pitch, which I have more than earned.

I opened up the text thread with my mother-in-law and sister-in-law. We've used it to plan surprises or gifts for Liv before, but I need it for something a bit extra today.

Me: SOS. I screwed up majorly last night because of a work commitment and I need to make it up to Liv. Is there a day this weekend when one of you could keep Annie for the night? If so I will kiss your feet and buy you something very expensive for your next birthday.

Andrea: If you agree to keep your mouth far away from my toes then yes, i would love to keep my niece on Saturday night.

Carla: Callum do not talk about feet. Very gross.

Every day I am thankful that I lucked out with my in-laws.

Me: Done. Mouth will stay a minimum of 100 feet from feet at all times.

Me: Seriously, I really appreciate it. I'm requesting PTO a few weeks from now so Liv and I can return the favor and keep all the cousins for a night or 2

Carla: Andrea, Grandma would love to stop by and make everyone dinner.

Andrea: I will take my shiny gift and the promise of childcare. What time do you want to drop her off?

Me: 7?

Andrea: Sounds good. What are you and Liv doing?

Me: Not sure yet, and looking to keep this a surprise from Liv. Messed up bad enough to need a gesture.

Carla: Best of luck, sweet boy.

With that taken care of, I switch over to my work email while I finish my coffee. Only 17 new emails since I stopped checking it yesterday. In all honesty, I left my phone in my office when I went to join everyone in the common area for happy hour. I wish I could say that I forgot but Liv's call yesterday freaked me out and the thought of coming home and having a scary conversation was the last thing that I wanted. Lately, all I want to do is come home, kiss my daughter, and snuggle up to my wife before passing out. I haven't gotten to do those things much recently because of work, but I know that we'll get back into it.

I have three separate emails from Emily, all about tweaks that we could make to our proposal. We're pitching our design, management, and consulting firm to CXE, one of the largest commercial real estate equity firms in our area. We want to show that we're ready to design, oversee, and then manage a portfolio of 11 different buildings through revitalization efforts and major construction projects. This would be a game-changer for me and the firm and would keep us busy and expanding for years.

I fire off a few quick responses to Emily with preliminary thoughts on the tweaks that she wants to make. She's been a real asset to me and this team since we brought her on. She was also at the happy hour last night where we spent most of the night talking about this project, meaning that she would have been up incredibly late to pitch me ideas with basic outlines and supporting figures. I checked and can see that the last email she sent came through at 2:17 am. I have got to give her a raise and then discuss the importance of proper sleep because I know that she'll also beat me to the office. Having someone who understands my drive and passion has been great, and I find myself leaning more and more on Emily for major parts of this project.

I assume that Jaime made a comment to my wife about Emily and the inside joke we have. Emily and I both know that it doesn't mean anything, just a fun way to rib each other about how much time we respectively spend at the office. I'm happy to call my boss my work grandfather, but somehow I don't think that it would go over as well with him. I'm also a bit annoyed at the idea of Jaime and my wife gossiping about one of my coworkers. On top of being new to our team, Emily is also young and that kind of gossip can travel back to the subject. That could result in an annoying HR situation for everyone, so I'll need to chat with Jaime today.

With that fun conversation on my mind, I put my empty coffee mug in the sink and head out the door.

NATURAL HISTORY (CALLUM)

Callum

"What's up?" Jaime stands in the doorway to my office, clad in her ever-present black suit and pumps. I swear, a black suit and heels are all that she's worn since we came into this firm.

"Can we chat for a second? Nothing bad, but we should close the door." A suspicious woman by nature, Jaime narrows her eyes at me before shutting the door and coming to stand near the corner of my desk.

"I'm just going to get straight into it because Liv and I talked about it this morning. Do you have an issue with the jokes that Emily and I make?"

She purses her lips for a moment before speaking, "Honestly Cal, I think that you need to be careful. I have seen the way Emily looks at you sometimes and I think that while you are in a stressful phase it's best to not send mixed signals to people that you could be attracted to."

"Do you think that I'm going to cheat on my wife? I love Liv and I would never do that to her. We have known each other since college, have you ever known me to be that kind of guy?" I'm incredulous because Jaime and I really have known each other for years, and hearing this from her hurts.

"I know that you love Liv and I am not saying that you're going to cheat on her. I do think that Emily seems to be interested in you, even if you don't see it. Sometimes you need to believe that other people are seeing things that you're not, Cal. I think that she's interested in you, and I think that you should be careful about the messages that you're sending."

"And maybe you need to be less sensitive about a joke that doesn't involve you. You upset Liv for no reason, and if you're having those same conversations with other people who work here then you'll also end up hurting Emily. She has been nothing but polite to you and it's unprofessional and, frankly, petty of you to start rumors about her."

"Why are you being so defensive over Emily and an unoriginal joke that no one else is in on? If it's just a joke, and it's causing issues with your wife, why not just stop saying it? Also, why is it so hard for you to conceptualize that I may see something that you don't? If we know each other as well as you were just saying, then you should know that I would never spread petty gossip or upset Liv unless I was legitimately concerned."

"I'm not going to go in circles with you, Jaime. You've made up your mind that I'm the bad guy and I'm not going to change your mind."

"That is so sanctimonious of you. You're avoiding this because I think you know there's truth to what I'm saying but fine, if you don't think we need to talk about then I won't waste my breath."

With that, Jaime swings out of my office, leaving me shocked at how that conversation went. I'm insulted that she seems to think there's something going on between me and Emily, and annoyed that she's making more out of this than there is. She's probably also stressed out about this pitch so I'll give her some leeway, but we'll have to talk about this again when she isn't so heated.

I look up when I hear a knock at my door, and ironically, it's the woman that my wife and friend have created issues over. Emily is a few years younger than me, but not by much. She is petite and keeps in shape; she'll always be the first to tell you about a workout she's doing or the health foods that she brings for lunch. It's never been my favorite topic of conversation, but I can smile and nod to be polite.

She has long dark that that's usually up and back, but she'll wear it down when we're at the happy hours or having lunch in my office. She's pretty enough, but she's no siren trying to tempt me from my marriage. She's a friend and quickly becoming one of my favorite colleagues. I decided then that distancing myself from her would just look suspicious and would actually make people think that we had something going on.

"Hey, office hubbs. Do you have a second? I was able to pull a few variance reports from the property on 2nd Street and I think we need to look again at the year-over-year engineering costs for the new builds. Do you have 20 or so minutes to work this out?"

"Sure, come on in. Thanks for pulling that. Do we have numbers for the properties over on Spring or 17th?"

And just like that, I am buried once again.

I set an alarm to make sure that I left on time, but then I had to stop by Emily's cubicle on my way out of the office to drop off materials that she had given me for feedback. Mostly everyone had left for the day, so Em's corner of the office was pretty quiet. I approach her from behind, and I wonder if she has a headache because her head is in her hands.

"Hey, you alright? Is the lack of sleep finally catching up?" When I start speaking, Em jumps up a bit and seems startled to see me.

She tries to duck her head, but I can see the red-rimmed eyes from here.

"Woah, Em. What's going on? Do I need to defend my work wife's honor?" She smiles at the corny joke, but it's a thin smile that drops pretty quickly.

"No need to beat anyone up, oh great protector mine. I think that I'm just still adjusting to the job switch. In my last role, I just met so many more people and I feel like I left a lot of friends to come here. Please don't misunderstand, I am grateful for the career advancement and I don't want to leave, but it is a big adjustment."

"Of course it is, and I totally get it. Technically working hours are over so no need to be too formal about it, I know that you like your job and you've been a huge asset to me so far. It's normal to have an adjustment period when you change jobs, and I hope that some of the team-building things that we're doing are helping. Are there other events or things that you did at your last office to help everyone get to know each other better?"

"Hmmm, I don't know. I do like the happy hours, but it can be overwhelming to happy everyone there. What if we did something smaller with just our team? Could help us all blow off a bit of steam."

"That's a good thought. I'll try to set something up next week before our pitch, and then we can plan something afterward. Now, I don't want to see any emails from you for the rest of the night. This will be here tomorrow, same as us. And then it'll be the weekend, and I don't want to see you working on anything unless something urgent comes up tomorrow. Got it?"

She gives me a feeble smile and says, "Got it. Nothing unless it's urgent."

We walk out together, and I make sure that she gets to her car safely before getting into my own to head home. The one nice thing about leaving the office as late as I have been lately is that I miss rush hour traffic by a few hours and it only takes me 20 minutes to get home.

I pull into our driveway and I can see that the girls played with the hose today. I smile thinking of them running around in the run and trying to spray each other. Maybe if I rush in I can see Annie before she goes to sleep.

It's dark when I walk in, and I drop my bag on the couch and creep down the hall to Annie's room. Liv leaves her door cracked so that Annie can get to us in case she has a bad dream, and I use that to my advantage so that I don't wake Annie by messing with any loud door handles. It's dark but for the ladybug nightlight plugged in near Annie's bed, and she's fast asleep. Her new dinosaur costume is on the little yellow beanbag chair in the corner and my heart aches for my sweet, strong daughter. I am missing so much of her life right now, but I have to remember that this is temporary and will benefit her in the long term.

I give Annie a quick kiss and then head back to the kitchen to unpack my lunch container and water bottle. I was for Liv to join me, as has become our routine for the last few weeks. She'll give me a basic rundown of the day while I reheat dinner or answer any client emails at our little kitchen table. She likes to find reasons to bump up against me in the cramped kitchen or give my butt a little pat. I had gotten all the way through my dishes with no sign of my wife before I headed back down to hall toward our room.

She's a lump under the sheets, and I can figure that she's dead to the world. By nature, my wife is a sleepy woman, and being a mom to our feral three-year-old has only put more demands on her. If I get a raise I should convince her to get a nanny, at least part-time. I have another lonely night ahead, and I just need to make it through tomorrow and then I can take the weekend to be with my girls.

"Why weren't we consulted about the date change when it was proposed?" I'm on the phone with one of our reps who's telling me that they want our full proposal, and an impromptu site visit to their corporate office two states over, a week earlier than agreed upon.

"Cal you know as well as I do that they're the client. This is also a big project for them and they're in the position to ask for whatever they want."

"I know, but this is wildly inconvenient. Obviously, we'll be there but I need to do a huge amount of schedule shifting to get our other pitch meetings moved or covered, travel arranged, and the proposal finished. I'm gonna let you go but yeah, we'll be there will bells on."

Thus, one of the more stressful Fridays of my life began. I get home late, even for me, and pass out on the couch the second that I get home. I don't even bother seeing if the girls are awake.

When I wake up on Saturday morning, I'm in an uncomfortably bent position on the couch, and for a moment I forget why I'm not in my comfortable bed. Then I hear the breakfast song coming from the kitchen and smell Annie's favorite apple pancakes that Liv makes. Unfortunately, I can smell my own breath so I sneak off to clean up before joining the girls.

I come out to the kitchen with a bear hug for my daughter locked and loaded, but I'm greeted by a sink full of dishes and an empty kitchen.

"Annie-saurus Rex? I have a pair of giant arms for you to borrow!" I call out to Annie and Liv as I move through the house and into the backyard, but then I look out the window and see that Liv's car is gone. Pulling out my phone, I call Liv.

"Hello?"

"Hey, I just got out of the shower and you all were gone. Did you run out for coffee or something? I was hoping that we could spend some time together today."

"We talked about this on Tuesday night. Andrea, Mom, and I are taking the kids out to the Natural History Museum. Remember? They have a new exhibit with dinosaur animatronics that we think Annie and the cousins might like."

I can hear Annie start to make dinosaur noises in the background.

"Why didn't you wake me up earlier? I could have gotten ready in time and gone with you."

"I told you on Tuesday that we had these plans and you didn't seem interested in going. I figured that was still the case when you got up and got in the shower. If you told me that you wanted to go I would have tried harder to wake you up."

I rub the ache forming behind my eyes. "I really wish you had reminded me about this. I've barely gotten to see you all and this would have been fun."

"Callum," Liv's voice has gone very quiet, "When I told you about these plans on Tuesday you said, and I quote "That will be fun for you all" while you answered emails. That did not make it seem like you were interested in going. I am also going to say that I am not your admin, and I have work and a child to manage. I cannot also remind you every time that we have plans."

"You're right, I'm frustrated with myself and it's not your fault."

"Besides, we can just see you after. Annie may need a short nap but maybe we can plan a garden party for this afternoon?"

"Yeah, I can't. This morning was the only time that I had free. We got a call yesterday that the client now wants us to fly out to do an in-person pitch, and they want us ready a week early. We're doing some emergency meetings at the office today and tomorrow to get everything done."

"Wow, that's hard. I'm sorry that plans are changing."

"Yeah."

Why am I having so much trouble walking to my wife? This is a stilted, formal version of us and I hate it. "Can you put me on speaker really quick? I want to say hi to Annie."

"Of course, give me one second." I hear some shuffling and then Live tells me I'm on.

"Where is my Annie-Saurus Rex? I want to hear her roar!" Annie bursts out into a fit of giggles and then gives me her best dinosaur roar, and we spend a few moments trading our sounds back and forth.

"Daddy, are you coming to see dinos wif me and Mama?"

"No baby, Daddy can't come. But he loves you very much and wishes that he could."

"But why daddy-," Liv butts in before Annie can go down a tantrum-inducing path of questions about why I'm not with her and her mom. "We're here! It is time to get baby dinos out of the car and into the museum!"

"Be safe, take pictures, I'll see you all later. Liv, I'm sorry but I have no idea when I'll be home."

"I figured. We've got a pretty good handle on the routine so need to worry about us." She didn't say it to hurt me, I'm sure of that, but the offhanded way that she told me not to worry makes my chest ache. They've adapted to me not being around and I hate it. We hang up and I throw on a more casual office outfit, figuring that if I can't see the girls I may as well just go to the office earlier than I planned and try to get home at a more reasonable time.

The entire team is coming in for the afternoon to do emergency pitch work and to complete work on projects that are getting moved for this bid. I send out the agenda before I leave the house, and Emily responds immediately. Even on the weekends, she beats me to the office. At least I won't have to be there alone.

Thanks for Dinner (Callum)

Callum

It's almost 6:00 before we come up for air. Jaime and the rest of the team are either out grabbing dinner or on a break; Emily and I have moved to one of the larger conference rooms to spread out and run through the deck on the large screen. The air of urgency we had this morning has eased a bit, now that we're all seeing the evidence of how hard we have worked on this pitch in the last few weeks. We're in a good place and everyone has been able to take their first deep breath since we heard that we needed to present this proposal in person and a week ahead of schedule.

"Thank you for what you said last week."

"Hmm?" I'm a bit absentminded when I reply to Emily, trying to think about the last time that I ate."

"My little meltdown that you caught. I appreciate that you were nice about it and didn't make anything weird." Emily seems almost shy, which is at odds with her usually confident personality.

"Don't worry about it. Changing jobs and then immediately jumping into a stressful project is rough."

"Either way, I just wanted to say thank you. You've really helped to make the transition easier." She puts her hand on my bicep and looks me in the eye to drive her point home.

"Hey," I hear from the doorway behind us. It catches me off guard and I jerk my arm from underneath Emily's hand before jumping out of my chair.

I turn to my wife, who standing in the doorway with a takeout bag. Her gaze jumps from me to Emily, who is still seated at the table.

"Am I interrupting? Jaime said that you all had broken for the night but I couldn't get ahold of you. I figured you were into something and would need dinner." She doesn't move to come any closer to me, and the distance feels cavernous, instead of a few feet.

"Of course not. Yeah, most people headed home and we were just getting ready to head out." I move towards her but before I can reach her she holds the takeout bag straight between us and I'm left with no choice but to take it and remain standing a foot or so away from her.

"Hi! I'm Emily, it's nice to meet you." Emily is standing beside me now and offering a wave to Liv.

Liv nods her head, "Ahh yes, it's very nice to meet you. Were you one of the people brought on for this project?"

"Yeah, it's been crazy but such a great opportunity. Working with Callum as much as we have been on this project has been great. It's nice to be in an environment with coworkers who are as intense and dedicated as he is, and who spend the necessary time to make these projects successful." I look down and Emily has her hand on my arm again. I subtly shift away under the pretense of moving the food bag to my other arm.

"Yes, he certainly is dedicated to his work. I'm glad to hear that he's been working with you. Callum has always been patient about helping people who need a little extra."

I frown at that because Liv's voice feels uncomfortably close to patronizing, and I don't like being discussed as if I'm not here. At the same time, there's something in the tone or body language between Liv and Emily that cautions me not to get in between them.

"Anyway, I'll head out. I also found this near the sink, and wanted to make sure that you had it."

Liv grabs something from her pockets and my face flushes. In her hand is my wedding ring, forgotten when I took it off to wash dishes this morning.

"You're married?" Emily asks me, almost accusingly, at the same time that I say, "I forgot to grab it after I showered." Liv raises her eyebrows at me and I can feel the flush on my face get worse.

"Yeah, I'm married. This is my wife, Liv, and I know that you've heard that name before." Everyone I work with knows about Liv, and most of them are friendly with her or ask me about her and Annie on a regular basis.

"Oh yeah, I think that I've heard your name from Jaime! I just didn't make the connection that you and Callum were also together."

"You didn't notice my ring?" There is no way Emily didn't know that I'm married.

"Not really. I really am sorry, it's just that most of the family guys keep pretty strict hours so I guess I just didn't think. Anyway, it was so nice to meet you Liv. It's really sweet that you brought dinner. See you later, Callum. I'll text you again if anything comes up but I'm feeling ready for this trip!" Emily gathers her bag and heads past Liv and out of the doorway.

There's more uncomfortable silence.

"How often are you forgetting your ring if she didn't even know that you're married?" I can see that Liv is hurt, and I need to squash this line of thought before it can go any further.

"I only take it off to protect it, Liv. I'm not sure how she didn't realize that I'm married, but it's not a secret and I'm sure that I've talked about you in front of her before. Maybe she's just tired, we've been at it all day."

"I'm sure that you have. Where is everyone else? I thought that you were all working today but Jaime said that she left an hour or so ago."

"Yeah, she was hungry and a few other people had to get home for family commitments that they couldn't break. Luckily we're at a really good spot and we all felt like we could call it a night, so I sent everyone home. I really only planned to stay and organize a few things."

"Everyone but Emily. Do you not consider yourself to be someone with family commitments?" Liv's arms are folded around herself and I know that I just stepped in it.

"I know that I'm someone with commitments, Liv. Not everyone has a wife like mine or a support system, and they don't have someone at home who can pick up their slack during these rough periods at work. Emily only stayed because she doesn't have a family or boyfriend and she's on some weird fasting diet so..." I trail off, hoping that Liv can see that I didn't orchestrate this situation to have alone time with Emily.

"How do you know that she doesn't have a boyfriend?" Liv's head is now cocked to the side.

"Huh?"

"You said that she doesn't have a boyfriend, how do you know that?" I can't get a handle on this conversation.

"It's just something that we talked about. Maybe she has one now, I don't know."

"You know that but she didn't realize that I'm your wife?"

"Liv, I don't know what she remembers or doesn't. I have a good memory, I remembered what she said in a conversation. I wasn't drilling her for her relationship status."

Liv looks away from me and then her head drops a bit and she starts slowly shaking her head. "I'm really tired, Callum. I don't know how much longer I can be the person who 'picks up your slack' at home.

I signed up to have a partner and I don't feel like I have that right now. Then coming in here and seeing how close you were sitting and how comfortable she is touching you makes me feel even less secure. It seems like you're separating into who you are at work and who you are at home, but the work version of you is bleeding into home and I don't know where my partner is."

"Liv, baby, I'm sorry that I've made you feel that way. I didn't realize when I was brought onto this what the hours would be like, but don't you see how much this could change things for us? You wouldn't have to work anymore, we could move into a bigger house before the next baby. And I'm sorry that it looked weird to you, but there is nothing going on between Emily and me."

"Jesus Christ, Callum!" Her sudden exclamation takes me off guard, such an alien reaction compared to how Liv usually speaks to me during disagreements. "The only reason you're mentioning the idea of a second kid is because you aren't an equal partner with the life we currently have.

"You're talking about a second baby and a bigger house because you aren't doing enough work with our family and home as it is. I'm sure that if I could just put it all into a box and know that someone else will automatically take care of things when I want to change my schedule, then I would want another baby too. But I don't have someone like that. You get to not worry about Annie or the house because it's an unspoken rule that I will trail behind you and pick up the pieces, or ease the path so that you can move forward in other parts of your life. When will I have someone who supports me like that?

"And why would I quit my job? Do you even know why I started working again?"

I'm stunned. All I can do is stare at my wife who is glaring my me, backlit by the sterile lighting in the empty office.

"I thought you started working because you wanted a bigger house so that we could have another kid."

"Callum, we talked about this and I told you that I started working because I missed the feeling of accomplishing something outside of being a mom. Did you think that I was lying or were you not listening?"

"I guess I- I mean that's just what I thought. I must have forgotten that conversation."

"Your memory is good enough to know Emily's relationship status but not good enough to remember the conversation we had about me wanting to achieve things outside of the home?"

I don't have anything to say to that, and Liv knows it. Once again, I'm just staring at my wife.

"Drive safe, enjoy dinner. Annie and I are staying with Andrea tonight."

I catch Liv's arm as she turns away from me to stomp out of the office. "Are you leaving tonight because you're mad at me? I already get so little time with Annie, I don't think that's fair."

"Don't talk to me about fair, Callum. And no, I asked Andrea to keep Annie so that we could have some time together tonight but I don't think that I can have a healthy conversation with you right now. If you want more time with Annie you'll have to figure it out, because I will not continue to uproot her schedule just to catch you for 20 minutes."

I follow behind Liv and watch her get into her car, wondering where I've gone so wrong. I thought that we were just going through a tough spot but that we were powering through because we knew how good it would be for our family. I thought that we were on the same page for our future but I didn't even know where my daughter was sleeping tonight.

CHAPTER 7: LIV

L^{iv}

When I hear the door unlock at 6:15 on Monday, I assume that Andrea is popping over to drop off something that Annie or I left at her house. When I instead hear the sounds of Callum and Annie greeting each other, I turn around in time to view the truly touching sight of my daughter greeting her father.

Callum was over the moon when he found out that he was going to be a "girl dad". I expected him to be excited about our baby but it seems like Annie being a girl put Callum over the edge into the obsessed category. He's the one who started buying all of the gender equality night time books and he would correct anyone who made overtly sexist comments about her. No one would get away with implying that Annie would be anything except strong and kind and whatever else she wanted to be.

Annie feels the same way about her father and I know that she's been missing him. I can see that him coming home on time is a step in the right direction, but Callum has a lot of work to do until I'm ready to move past these last few months.

I spent a lot of time talking this out with Andrea and then writing out all of my feelings about our relationship. Our marriage has been put under external pressure in the last few months and it has revealed that Cal and I aren't as in-sync as I previously assumed that we were.

There's the obvious issue of most of the house and child care being thrust onto me, but in hearing his justification it also seems like we aren't aligning on what we think our material needs are. Cal kept coming back to how much this would improve our financial standing and how I wouldn't have to work or we could upgrade the house, but I would trade a beach house for a solid marriage in a second.

We have a few long and probably uncomfortable conversations in front of us, but I'm still feeling too hurt to have them constructively. I refuse to fight with Cal just for the sake of my anger. That isn't the marriage that we have, and that's not the person that I am.

All the same, I feel so much comfort in Cal being home at a more regular time. Annie does a fantastic job of filling my time, but when she goes to bed I just feel so lonely without my husband. I clean the house, check in on Annie, and then I end up just roaming around the house trying to find something to do. I usually workout in the morning and my body is exhausted by the evening, but my mind isn't quite ready to go down yet.

Cal and I used to fill that time doing all of the mundane tasks that are required when you're adults and parents. Dishes, laundry, and toy repair were just so much easier when I wasn't doing it alone. We would make it a game or share flirty glances and playful touches. But lately I drag my feet on all of it and the tasks that used to make me feel like I'm part of a team make me feel like a single parent.

Annie pulls Cal over to her toy bin, but he asks her to pick out a toy while he says hi to me. I'm brought nearly to tears when he gathers me to him, tucking his head into my shoulder and just letting me feel how solid he is. My arms hang by my slides for a moment until my brain kicks in, and I bring my hands up to his shoulders and hold him impossibly harder to me.

We may not be on solid ground right now, but I know this man. I know his mind, his body, and his spirit. My eyes start to burn with the rush of emotion from this moment of reconnection. Neither one of us says anything and we stay locked like that until little hands start slapping at our legs.

I let loose a laugh and a sob all at once when Cal brings Annie into his arms and resumes the hug, although much more light-hearted than our charged embrace of a moment ago. Eventually I turn around to finish dinner and we have the most regular, boring evening together that shows me we'll move in the right direction as long as we're moving together.

Cal and I are still quiet when we get into bed that evening. I had the chance to take an extra long shower and to do a bit of journaling when Cal put Annie down, and I feel more prepared to talk to Cal about what's been going on.

It's as if we both knew that we were waiting for a peaceful moment to talk, and he twists his torso towards me at the same time that I twist towards him.

"So-," we share a smile when we speak at the same time, and he nods his head to tell me to go first.

"Thank you for coming home earlier tonight. I know that Annie loved it, but I also really enjoyed having you with us tonight."

"I feel awful that you have to thank me for being home at a reasonable hour or for spending time with you and Annie. After you left and I had the house to myself for the night, it started to really click for me how much time I've been spending away from you. I hated being here without you. It was quiet and cold and I feel awful that you might have felt that way."

"I did feel that way, for a while. Thank you for apologizing, and I know that you love me and Annie, but I think that we have a larger issue on our hands. I am ... bothered, I guess, that I felt like I was telling or showing you what I needed, and you just didn't pick up on it or listen. I know that we talked about going back to work, I know that I mentioned how exhausted I've been taking on more at home and with Annie. Why do you think those messages weren't getting across?"

"I don't really know, to be honest with you. I feel like I can't quite get my bearings and it all feels a bit off center right now. I honestly don't remember those conversations, which I guess doesn't make it any better."

"It doesn't, Cal. We've grown so far apart in such a short amount of time and that's really concerning to me. I feel like I got shut out of your decision making process. You decided that our family needed this big promotion, but we never talked about why you feel that pressure. Having things isn't as important to me as having you and Annie close. I respect that you have a drive to be successful at your job, but I will not accept a part time father or partner. Not to mention, you aren't sleeping enough or taking care of yourself. I love you too much to be complicit while you work yourself to the bone over a promotion that we don't absolutely need."

Cal takes a minute to digest what I'm telling him, and his mouth thins a bit.

"I don't think I see us as that weak, Liv. It has been, undeniably, a rough couple of months but it was never my intention to be a part time anything to you or Annie. I wish that I could stay home with the two of you everyday, but we can't be too secure in anything and I don't want to put us in a position of having to make major sacrifices down the road. What I'm doing right now - the long hour and shitty diet and time away from you - is to make your lives better and I guess I feel like the years behind us should show you that this is temporary. I'm struggling with the feeling that you have these major doubts about my commitment to you or Annie because I don't think that I deserve that."

It's my turn to take a beat so that I don't react too emotionally to what he said. I need to be delicate but strong about all of this, and that tightrope feels impossibly taught right now.

"I am not trying to criticize and I'm sorry if I'm coming across that way, but please understand that I am trying to show you how deeply hurt I am. I know that you love me and Annie, but we need your time and attention to feel it. When things started to get hard you just stopped talking to me, and stopped listening when I tried to bring it up. You've said yourself that you don't even remember some of those big conversations that we've had. If we're not communicating then nothing is going to change and I am justified in telling you that I'm hurt by a lot of this.

"You have always been an active father, which is why I got whiplash when you made a decision to put us through this "temporary phase" without telling me what it would entail. This isn't about credit or the past, it's about cracks that are forming right now."

"I didn't even really know! I can't tell you if I don't know it either. We brought on so many new people who had to be trained and so much fell on me to make sure that everything went smoothly. I spend all of my time at work trying to solve issues and manage people, and I guess that I just used all of that energy there. I am so drained when I come home that I dread the start of the next day."

"It's awful that you feel that way, but I didn't know because you didn't tell me. From my perspective, my husband and partner just all of the sudden had this big project that took him away all the time, and now there is some other woman who gets all of his emotional energy."

"Don't make it sound like that. Liv. There's no other woman who is getting anything from me. E know that Emily was a bit weird when you met her but consider that she came into this and had to immediately jump on this project. You know what it's like to be young and having to meet new people."

"Why are you being defensive over her? She was intentionally rude to me when we met, and she made sure to imply that I'm not important to you."

"Might I add that you were not particularly kind. I've seen you meet my coworkers and never once have you implied that any of them need "extra help" because we have a lot of meetings together. You took her off guard."

"Do you hear yourself? Are her feelings really that much more important to you than mine?"

"None of this is about Emily, and it's ridiculous for us to get side-tracked on something that doesn't matter. We're having problems between the two of us, and you bringing her into it isn't helpful. We are the ones who need to communicate and prioritize our marriage, everyone else is a non-factor."

"Except that I don't think that's true. I'm not saying that you're in love with her or that anything is going on, but I think that the way she acted towards me should show you that she's to the idea."

"And I'm not. We need to get back to our issues, Liv. I don't want to keep talking about her."

"Fine, then what's going to change? How are we going to make sure that we're actually talking to each other? I don't know how else to reach you, Cal. I know that this project is temporary, but if we set a precedent that we stop talking to each other when one of us gets overwhelmed then we're going to have this argument over and over again until we just stop arguing or speaking to each other all together."

We're both quiet for a moment, and everything that we've said makes the air between us feel as thick as smoke.

"When you go on your trip, I think that we need to be intentional about this time away. I get that you'll be thinking about this meeting, but I need to feel like you're thinking about us, as well. I admit that I need to sort out some of my feelings as well, so maybe I'll write them all down and have a better grasp of them after. I don't want to argue with you Cal, but I'm also tired. I need you to put just a bit of energy into this while you're away."

"Of course, of course, baby. I also hate arguing with you, and I think that you're right. I'll take some time and maybe I'll try to take your approach and write some things down."

We both can feel that a bit of progress has been made, and there's some semblance of a plan for us. When we're flying down I reach my hand out to Cal, and he squeezes it a moment before kissing my knuckles and then rolling over. I slept well next to my husband, for the first time in a while.

CHAPTER 8: CALLUM

C allum

I take my first unburdened lungful of air in two months. The pitch is done. It went well and we had the figures to back up what we proposed, but even if the firm isn't awarded the contracts, I get to close this season of my life. I can go back home knowing that I did what I needed to do, and continue to improve my marriage.

I smile to myself when I think about being home for all of Annie's nighttime routines, and the pleasure of an unrushed morning. Liv and I are still taking time to separately reflect on our relationship, and I've written her a few letters during this trip. I don't know if she'll ever read them, but carving out time to center myself and really be introspective about my relationship with my wife has given me a degree of clarity about the entire situation.

My musings are interrupted by the voices of my team around me, and I become aware that I've just been staring out of the window of the SUV that we rented for this trip.

"What do you think, Cal?"

"Huh?"

When I look back, I can see Emily and Jaime looking at me expectantly.

"I said," Emily throws back with a sarcastic eye roll, "that we've all earned a night to let loose a little bit. I have a college friend who owns a really nice lounge downtown and she said that we should stop by."

I look at Jaime, who shrugs. "I texted everyone else and they're down. We have plenty of time to head back to the hotel to take a break and then change before we leave, and we have the car through tomorrow so we may as well use it. Can everybody be ready by 8?"

"As long as everyone knows that this won't be a company tab and that we have an early flight tomorrow, that's fine."

When we pull up to the hotel I head over to the bar. If I go to my room I'm going to pass out and I want to write out my notes and impressions on the meeting. There were a few projections that the CXE team asked about and I have thoughts that I didn't touch on during the meeting. I'm going to send them a follow up, as I would with other clients, and offer to expand upon those specific points.

A body lands next to mine at the bar, and I look over to see Jaime veering for the elevator banks and Emily sliding into the seat next to me.

"Need to unwind before tonight?" She asks while waving the bartender over.

"Not yet, I have a few thoughts about the meeting that I want to get down before we leave." I open up my computer to makes notes on the slide deck that we used.

"I really admire how dedicated you are to this, Cal. It's been incredible to be so close to you and to learn from you."

I'm not sure what to do with that statement. Overt compliments have always made me feel a bit awkward.

"Thank you, but I think it's just about finding work that you're motivated to do. I work to live, not the other way around, but I like a job where I can take initiative and get to implement a level of creativity into my work."

Emily turns to the bartender, "Can I get a double gin and tonic and then a double whiskey sour for him? Thanks."

"Oh, I think it's a bit too early for me to be drinking," I say, but the bartender has already moved on to make our drinks.

"You've earned it! And besides, it'll go on my tab. I get what you're saying about work vs. life, but I definitely think that you're a little more work oriented than you think. But that's an amazing quality, some people just don't have the drive to really go after what they want. I think that you and I are similar. We know what we want and we make it happen."

The bartender breaks our eye contact by placing our drinks down, and I use mine as an excuse to look away from Emily. The woman really can be intense, and I never quite know how to handle it.

"Hey, thanks for the drink but I'm getting a bit of a headache so I'm going to head upstairs and rest before we go out. I'll see you down here at 8?"

I gather my laptop and finish my drink because hey why waste a drink that someone is already paying for.

"Sure! I'll be down. If you want to meet up early or start down here just text me." She gets up and hugs me unexpectedly.

I just nod and head to the elevator banks. When I get up to the floor that we're all on I pull out my phone to call Liv.

"So how'd it go?" She answers the phone eagerly and it makes me happy to know that she was probably thinking of me.

"It went well, but I'm ready to never have to worry about it again. If we get the contract it'll be great, but if we don't get it I will still get my life back. I miss you, baby, you and Annie. Do you think that we should try to take a trip soon? I can put in for leave and if you can get away from work, even just a staycation weekend nearby, I'd be over the moon."

I've flopped down on the bed, and I feel like a teenager talking to his crush, except that this woman is my wife and I don't have to drive her home before curfew.

"I think that would be great, actually, and I was going to suggest pretty much the same thing. I'm glad that we got some of this out before you left, but I miss you and I want to continue making our marriage a priority. I don't want to go through this again."

"I agree. Look, I'm going to write down a few meeting notes and then take a nap before we all go out for drinks tonight. Can I call you later?"

"Sure. Who all is going out for drinks?"

"It'll be the whole team. It turns out that Emily has a friend who owns a lounge downtown. No clubbing or bar hopping, just some unwinding."

"Okay. Please just be ... I don't know, aware? I get that you don't see it but I really do think that Emily is doing more than sucking up to her boss."

"And if she were trying more, I would have to be receptive, which I'm not. I get that you see something different but please just trust me. I'll be with Jaime all night and I'll call you when I get back, okay?"

"Alright. I love you."

"Love you, too."

After we hang up I change out of my suit, lay my jeans out for later, and crawl into bed. The call with Liz nags at me a little, not letting me sleep. When I get back we're going to need to add a section to our conversations about trusting me. I've never done something to give Liv an actual reason to be suspicious, and I admit that it's insulting to feel like I'm defending myself to my own wife.

I'm not one of those husbands and we aren't one of those marriages.

CHAPTER 9: LIV

L^{iv}

Cal and Jaime both told me that they were leaving the hotel around 8, and Jaime and I chatted about the plan for the evening when she FaceTimed me to show me her outfit and complain about a guy that she's been seeing. Cal told me that he'd check in with me when he gets back, so I figure it'll be late. Annie and I go through our evening routine, and when she's down for the night I edit a few projects and then send them to a client of mine.

I don't want to fall asleep and miss Cal's call, because I'll take any chance for us to connect, even for just a few minutes. I end up looking at a few spas close to us, for when Cal takes some time off. I'll make sure that we take a few days with Annie and do all of the family things together, but Annie is happiest when her parents are happiest. And Annie's parents are happiest when they're together.

I end up picking two staycation packages that I think we would like, and three family packages. When Cal gets home we can sit down and decide which one we want. We're finally moving forward together and while I know we aren't out of the woods yet, I can see the light at the end of the tunnel. I can see us in 6 months and I just know it's going to be completely different.

I do end up dozing on the couch, but I'm awake enough to get Cal's call right before midnight.

"Hey! How was the lounge?"

There's a pregnant pause, and time starts to stretch. I'm not sure how I know, but something is wrong. My face feels hot, my throat clogged, and I wait for Cal to tell me that he's back at the hotel and ready to get home.

But that's not what he tells me.

"I'm so sorry, Liv. Baby I am so sorry. I love you so much and I don't know what happened."

"Tell me. I need you to say it, Cal."

"I - me and Emily - we... I'm so sorry."

I'm sitting up now, on the squishy couch that we've had since before Annie was born. We were talking about upgrading to a nicer sectional, but with just the three of it it felt wasteful. Plus, this is the couch that we bought when we moved into this house. The couch that our family sat on when we announced our engagement, our pregnancy. I nursed Annie on this couch, Cal cradling us between his legs during our night time feeds because I couldn't always stay awake on my own.

It's seen better days, but something in me just wasn't ready to part with it. Now, though, I want to walk to the kitchen, grab our longest serrated bread knife, and filet it into unrecognizable strips of fabric and stuffing. Then I want to take those pieces into the front yard and burn them. I want the entire neighborhood to see the black plumes from burning polyester and years of stains; they'll smell years of spilled drink and dinner parties and our messy baby. I want them to come out of their houses and linger on the sidewalk in front of our yard while the evidence of our lives together burns, until the ashes leave a scorch in the soil that will never again bear so much as a weed.

I need someone to witness this pain, because without an audience I have nothing. I have misery on an old couch that should have been tossed years ago. I have a sobbing husband on the phone asking me to say something, to make him feel better for what he's done to our lives.

"I told you. I told you so many times and you wouldn't listen. Why wouldn't you listen to me?"

In contrast to Cal's sobbing, I sound calm. I can hear myself, but almost as if I'm hearing someone else. Some other wife is having this conversation with her husband. I'm just watching from my old couch, observing from outside of myself.

"I don't know! It just happened. I don't know why I did it, but it meant nothing. We didn't go all the way and I-"

"Didn't go all the way? What are you, 15? Do you think that I really care about the degree to which you cheated on me? Do you want me to tell you that makes it better? Oh gee, baby, I'm so happy that you didn't fuck that other woman that I don't care about the rest of it! Get real."

"I wouldn't do that to you. It was one time, I swear, nothing has happened and I stopped it from going any farther."

"How many times do you think I've cheated on you, Cal?"

"I - what?"

"How many times do you think that I've cheated? If we're keeping score, even though it was only once, as you say, then you're still ahead. Somehow I've managed to maintain my vows to you, my promises. I have protected our relationship while you throw it around like something you've bought in the dollar bins."

"Please, Liv. We'll go to therapy, I'll quit my job! I'll send the email now and send it to you so that you can see. We have savings, so when I come home I can just be with you and Annie for a few months. We can fix this."

"I have been asking you to fix this, to work on this with me for months and you would not listen. You can do what you want, and obviously you have, but from here on out the relationship you should worry about fixing is the one you have with your daughter. I am not your wife or your partner anymore. We won't be friends, we won't celebrate each other's birthdays. I might just forget when yours is."

It's November 14th, and I already picked out what I was going to get him. Cal wants us to get into hiking so I found some outdoor adventuring classes for us to take and we would have had a great time. Maybe he can take Emily, since for all I care he can go live in a tent.

"Please just don't make any decisions until I come and we talk about this. I love you so much, I'm serious I'll do anything you need. Just let me try. You don't have to do it anymore, I'll do all the work."

"Trust me Cal, I've been on that side and it's no way to live. When you get back I'm sure we'll talk about this more."

I hang up on him, which is a first for me. His voice was just grating at my ears and the time-worn polyester of the couch suddenly feels like sandpaper. The lights on the appliances are too bright. My skin feels wrong. Itchy. My insides are too big for my body. I am seeping out of every one of my pores until the newly liquid parts of me stain in the hardwood. This feeling will stay in this house and warp the wood of the flooring for the new owners.

But none of that is happening. I am standing in my living room and my husband is texting me, calling me. He just told me that he cheated on me and I can hear the warm sloshing of the dishwasher. I can see a car drive past our front window. I can smell the lavender of the cleaning products that I use.

I'm in my home and I'm a mother, and I need to go to sleep. This will all be here tomorrow, but there will be no trace of the family who used to live in this house.

CHAPTER 10: CALLUM

A /N: Wow, thank you for such a wonderful response to the chapters so far! I always appreciate the kind and constructive comments. There are emotional scenes and chapters in the pipeline, but this one may not be satisfying for those looking for an immediate blow up.

I'm always interested in characters as individuals, and I believe that people deserve development even when they aren't perfect. Infidelity happens for a myriad of reasons, and these characters are going to go through a lot in the next 10 or so chapters. Rest assured, Olivia will get her moment and Callum will continue to come to terms with the situation that he has created for himself and his family.

Callum

Have you ever stayed underwater for too long? For the first 10 seconds you're fine, and then your brain starts to send alert signals and you begin to panic. If you know what you're doing, you can train your brain to relax, to not panic and to stay calm.

When I was on the swim team in high school, they made us do a lot of breathing drills and taught us techniques for breath holding without panicking. For a while there I could go about 2 minutes without oxygen, and I started to implement those breathing exercises to keep me calm in other aspects of my life.

None of those techniques work for me now, and I've been stuck in those first 10 seconds of panic since I called my wife and told her that I cheated on her. I can't breathe, can't think about anything except for what I've done to my life. Will I have a wife to come home to? I don't want to harass Liv so all I've texted her is that I love her, I'll do anything that she needs me to do, and then I told her when I expect to be home.

Looking at my phone, it's obvious that she doesn't want to text me this morning. Can't blame her because I don't particularly want to know myself either. Instead, I call Jaime and hope that she won't kill me, for waking her up earlier than necessary and for what I have to tell her.

"What?" She's obviously groggy, but I need to get this over with.

"It's Cal. Can you meet me at the cafe downstairs?"

"Cal I really don't think that we need to start working at," the phone rustles as I assume she puts it down to look at the clock, "Jesus Christ! 5:18 in the morning. Even for you that's unnecessary."

"It's not about work Jaime. It's about last night and I need to talk to you."

"I'll be down in 5 minutes." And the line goes dead as she hangs up. Does she have an inkling as to what I'm going to tell her?

This is going to be humiliating, but I need to get it over with. If I did it, I need to be able to tell the people that I respect and accept those consequences. I get down to the lobby cafe first and order mine and Jaime's coffee. I'm staring at the cup, letting the warmth seep into my cold hands, but I can't bring myself to drink. My throat is tight and I'm pretty sure that anything I try to eat today will just come right back up.

"What happened," Jaime asks before she's even sitting.

I need to rip off the Band-Aid, to tell Jaime so that she can be ready for Liv. I know that I can't be my wife's emotional rock through this, but maybe I can give her someone else. Selfishly, I also need to talk to someone. I need someone who knows us, knows our relationship, to tell this to. I take a deep breath before allowing it to come out, knowing that I may be losing one of my oldest friends in the next few seconds.

"I cheated on Liv last night. With Emily. Liv knows and I think that she'll need you when we get back. I have no idea what's going to happen with us but she'll need you and Andrea to be there for her."

Jaime just nods, then looks down at her coffee. She blows on the surface, not looking at me and just digesting what I've told her. My stomach roils while I wait.

"I really, really wish that I could say I was surprised. Six months ago I would have been shocked but not as much now."

"I don't know what happened, Jaime. I really don't understand why I did it."

"I have some ideas, but I want to know what, exactly, happened last night between you and Emily?"

"I think that Liv should be the first to know."

"I think that the time for talking to Liv about what's going on between you and Emily has passed. I want to know what happened, that way I can make sure that you tell her the truth if she wants it down the road."

I nod, knowing that her lack of faith in me is fair. I haven't earned trust from the people in my life and that is going to be a hard pill to swallow. I scrub my hands down my face, hoping that it grounds me even a little. Instead, all I feel is old stubble and puffy eyes.

"I swear that this was the first and last time that anything has happened between me and Emily. This wasn't planned, and I haven't thought about being with her like that. Maybe I realized that she has a crush on me, but I figured it was just a passing thing. I'm the only one at the firm that she really hangs out with at work, and it's natural for some flirting to happen. I-" Jaime cuts me off.

"You're stalling and you're justifying it, Cal. If Olivia ever wants to have this conversation with you she isn't going to want to hear about all the ways that you think it isn't that bad. Just tell me what happened last night."

"We had a drink at the hotel bar after the pitch, but I finished it quickly and then went upstairs to call Liv. Then I laid my clothes out and took a nap. I met you all downstairs in the lobby, and you know what happened from there. Car, lounge, getting a table. Emily and I started talking about the pitch, and then her last workplace. She started talking about an ex and she was working with, and then a bad boss she had.

"Fuck, looking back on it now, I can see that she was using those guys to flatter me. We all had a few rounds of shots and then you went to dance. The guys went to grab something to eat at the bar. That left Emily and I at the table."

The worst part is coming up, the part that makes me glad I didn't try for breakfast. I can see it all happening like I'm watching a movie, and I'm screaming at the main character not to be such a fucking idiot. Not to ruin his life.

"I got up to go to the bathroom, and then I felt someone grab my arm in the hallway. I swear, swear to you that I didn't realize she followed me. I was pretty drunk, I know that we all were, but I only got up to go to the bathroom. I turn around and she's on me, kissing me and has her hands on my chest. Something just...clicked, I guess in my brain and I responded. I pushed her against the other wall and practically mauled her. It wasn't until she, um, fuck." My hands are in my hair and I wish that I could just yank it all out.

"It wasn't until her hands were in my pants that I realized what we were doing. It all happened so fast and I know that it was some combination of alcohol and stress and missing Liv. I don't want to be with Emily, I never have and I never will. I just want my family and I have no idea why I did it. It was just an instinctual thing and when I realized what I was doing I stopped and took a cab back here. It's why I didn't ride back with you all."

"Do you think that this is some complicated issue? Cal, I can see exactly how this happened and it's a tale as old as time. One," she holds up a finger to indicate that she's going to be listing something off, "you liked the ego boost of a younger woman who liked you.

I believe that you may not have romantic feelings for her, but you obviously liked the way it felt to have her interested in you.

"Two, you ignored me and your wife when we told you what we were seeing because you didn't want to admit that this was an exercise in vanity. And three, somewhere along the way you have stopped thinking of yourself as part of a family unit. You've prioritized your need to feel wanted and you thought that you could control yourself, but you were wrong.

"People who "only want their families" don't act like that. I don't know what is next for you but you really need to get yourself figured out. I still love you, because you are one of my oldest friends, but I don't like you very much right now and I am so wildly disappointed in the decisions that you've been making."

She hasn't broken eye contact with me and hearing that she still loves me breaks the damn. Tears start again, despite me feeling as if I emptied the well last night. I can't refute what she's said because having it all laid out for me like that is sobering and it brings things into perspective. If one of the other guys on the team did this then I would tell him the same things that Jaime is telling me now.

I reach across the table and grab Jaime's hand, desperate for some sort of connection with my friend.

"What do I do? Last night she sounded like she was done with me and I don't know how to handle that."

"You figure out how to handle it and don't put anything else on her. I've never cheated on my wife so I don't know what to tell you, but you'll need to be ready to take what she gives you." She squeezes my hand for a moment before releasing it and rising from her seat, grabbing her room card on the way up.

"I meant what I said, Cal. I still love you and care about you, but I need to support Liv. Does she know that you told me?"

I shake my head.

"My last piece of advice is to not tell anyone else until she's ready or asks you to. You should follow her lead on how much you tell people, because it can be uniquely humiliating for the women who are cheated on. I'm going to finish packing, but I'm serious about figuring out why you changed, Cal. I don't know if that's therapy or something else, but Annie and Liv deserve more than a husband or father who can't control himself. So do you."

I sit in the cafe for a while after she leaves, digesting what she told me. I'm ashamed of a lot of things right now, but the knowledge that everyone else could see what was happening makes me feel even worse, like the most predictable cliche. I dug my heels in about a woman who doesn't mean anything to me, and it's cost me every-thing.

CHAPTER 11: LIV

A/N: This chapter is shorter, as this week and next week are fairly busy between my regular work and social life. Thank you for all of the kind and encouraging comments, and hopefully this chapter has slightly better editing!

Liv

I feel bad about how much I've been leaning on Andrea lately, but I know I'll return the favor eventually. The great thing about sisters is that, as much as I've tormented her and as many of my sweaters as she's stolen, she was my first call in the morning and immediately knew that something awful had happened. When I started telling her, she made me stop, and then she was at my house with coffee, breakfast, and her husband and kids in no time.

She assumed that I would be packing my things, but Cal can go screw himself if he thinks I will be the one to leave. Annie and I did nothing wrong, and there is no reason why we should have to uproot our lives more than necessary. My first preference would be to have him out of our home, out of my life, and scrubbed from the last 10 years of my memories.

In the interest of Annie, however, I don't shred all of her father's clothes, books, and clutter. Instead, I tell her that mommy and daddy are going to have their own rooms now, just like her. We have a small office/guest room with a pull-out bed, and I hope that Cal gets an incurable neck problem from the cheap mattress.

I'm grasping for petty or angry energy, but it fades pretty quickly. Well, it fades for me, at least, but Andrea has no problem suggesting my next steps. I could email Cal and Emily's HR department, I could go scorched earth and tell him that we'll only talk through our lawyers, I could take him for every penny and leave him destitute.

I have a feeling that's not going to happen, though because every sweater of his that I pick up smells like him. It smells like the woodsy cologne that I started buying for him after our first anniversary. The pictures on the walls still show the face of a man that I loved - still love - looking back at me. I'll see that face when I look at Annie, or remember the last decade of my life. None of that goes away because the man that I love cheated on me.

Our love used to feel warm, reliable, passionate, heady, but now it feels like a curse. Like a slug that crawled into my head and whispers at me from inside myself.

What if this has been going on for months? What if she's not the first or only? What if I can never find love like this again?

Ultimately, none of that is helpful. I accept that I still love my husband, I accept that he's done this, but that doesn't mean that I will accept him back into our home or my heart. I won't. I refuse to show Annie that this is an acceptable way to treat someone that you love.

I need time to figure out how to move forward with my life, so I ask Andrea and her family to head home and bring Annie with them. Andrea has been on a warpath this morning, as has her husband, but anger feels like sawdust in my mouth. My brain is coming to terms with my reality, but my body is behind and speaking about him like that feels wrong.

All of a sudden I'm looking down at our bed, covered in Cal's stuff, and a wave of exhaustion hits me like a Mack truck. I've already pulled his knickknacks out of our bookshelf, his toiletries out of the bathroom, and cleared out his bedside table. The constant motion was helpful when I woke up this morning, but the next thing I know I'm on the floor. Why should I be exhausting myself to make his transition easier?

I have allowed myself to fall into this role of domestic martyr lately, and it's eating me from the inside out. This is the time to force myself to put it down and let Callum deal with the fallout of his choices.

I move into the living room to grab my cell, and I can see a text from Cal telling me when he'll be home. I realize that he'll be back in about 20 minutes, and I don't want to see him for the first time after he cheated on me looking like a wreck. I might not have the energy to go over my feelings with Andrea, but I have enough stored up to take a shower, blow-dry my hair, and change out of my pajamas because I'll be damned if I look like the jilted wife on a 90's harlequin romance cover.

The scalding water of the shower turns my skin pink, aided by the aggressive scrubbing of my washcloth. I give up when I realize that I can't clean my body enough to rid myself of this feeling. I go through the motions of my regular routine, taking note of how much extra counter and cabinet space I'll have in my bathroom from now on. When I grab a comfortable pair of linen slacks and a bodysuit, I think that maybe I'll go to Ikea and get new shelves so that I can move my shoes into the space that's been freed up in my closet.

I'm in the kitchen making tea when I hear the door open and Cal's keys hit the glass bowl on the entryway table. I used to get so excited when I would hear him come home, and Annie and I would rush to the front of the house to greet him when he came home. He would throw her up into the air and give her a raspberry then pull me in for a kiss.

But now I remain in the kitchen, and I make no move to go to him. Since he called me last night and told me what he had done, I've been primarily thinking of the future in terms of a few hours. What I need to pack, how I'll explain the immediate changes to Annie, and who to call first. Now that those decisions have been made, I'm flooded with an odd sense of calm for the coming storm. Callum made his choices already, and he's an adult who can handle the consequences.

"I'm in the kitchen," I call out to him, voice level and calm even to my ears.

His steps stutter before he walks through the living room and sees me at the other side of the counter, stirring our favorite floral honey into a green tea.

It feels like there's a stranger in my home. This man looks like my Cal, is wearing a suit that I helped my Cal pick out, but the man looks exhausted and defeated. He doesn't come to me or make any moves forward.

I won't make this easy for him just because he looks sad.

Instead, I pull my mug up to my mouth and blow over the surface before taking a sip. "So, honey, how was your trip?"

CHAPTER 12: CALLUM

A/N: Thank you for being patient with me on chapter updates! I know it's hard to have to wait when we've just entered the betrayal, but real life is quite busy right now. Enjoy!

Callum

This morning, I emailed everyone, telling them I needed to run a few documents over to the CXE office. In reality, it's because I can't bring myself to even look at Emily. It's not that I can't be trusted around her; it's that thinking about her makes me feel ill. So, instead of forcing myself to be around her and pretending I didn't betray my wedding vows with her last night, I changed my flight information and gave myself a few extra hours to examine this situation from every angle.

I've been jittery since it happened, but I need to pull myself together if I'm going to save my marriage. There isn't a world worth living in where my wife doesn't love me, but I never thought we'd be in this position, and I'm not 100% sure how to tackle this problem. I know that Liv needs to see that I'm ready to put in the work to fix our marriage and earn back her trust, so I write down everything I can think of before I get home.

I wish I could tell Liv that everything was one-sided, but my wife isn't an idiot. Despite what she, admittedly, has reason to believe, I haven't been deaf to her complaints about Emily and my work schedule. Truthfully, I think I brushed them off because I resented that she thought so little of me. I've never been unfaithful before, never given her a reason to distrust me, and it was insulting that she was constantly implying that I wasn't dedicated to my family, that I didn't miss the time I used to spend with them. I thought I was doing this big thing to make our lives better in the future, but, in reality, I think I've been ignoring what was obvious to everyone else.

I know I love my wife; I know I don't want to be with anyone else and can't picture a life with anyone but her. Unfortunately, I lulled myself into a false sense of entitlement and confidence, stopped listening to the one person whom I have always trusted in the past.

These realizations may be coming a day late and a penny short, though. I spend the entire flight writing things down; things I need to apologize for, things I don't have answers for yet, and things I'll do to regain Liv's trust. I want to have all my thoughts and plans well laid out before I see my wife.

The closer my car gets to the house, the harder my clammy hands grip the wheel. At this point, I'm fairly confident I'm going to leave sweaty indents in the leather of the steering wheel. Will Liv even be at the house? She and Annie could be at Andrea's or even a hotel. It doesn't matter because I'll scour this town until I find her and bring her home.

I'm relieved to see her sedan in the driveway. I know it's a bit much, but I park in a way that she won't be able to get out of the driveway without moving my car first. She's never shied away from an argument before, but we've never had to work through something of this magnitude.

Everything looks normal when I walk in; I don't see any moving boxes, and our wedding photo is still blown up above the mantle. I wait for a moment and listen to the house, but I can't hear anything other than the normal hums and creaks of our home. The girls usually meet me at the door, but that doesn't happen today.

I pause in the entryway, waiting to hear some signs of life in the house.

After a beat, I hear, "I'm in the kitchen," and steel myself for what is coming next. It's as if I've passed into the twilight zone when I walk into the kitchen and see my wife at the counter, asking me how my business trip went. She's never called me 'honey' before. She's never waited in the kitchen for me when I got home, and it feels like there's a different woman who looks just like Liv.

Muscle memory means I've already shed my keys, luggage, and blazer at the front door. I'm standing in front of my wife in travel-wrinkled slacks and a button-down with coffee splatters from an overpriced airport coffee. On the other hand, Liv looks gorgeous, if not tired. The dark rings under her eyes and the tense way she holds her body show me that she probably didn't sleep much better than I did.

"Is Annie here?" I ask her. Whatever this conversation is, Annie shouldn't have to hear it. Liv should be able to say whatever she needs to say without having to worry about little ears. She's young, but Annie is old enough to sense that her parents are fighting, and Liv and I have always been intentional about how we communicate when Annie isn't here.

Liv raises her eyebrows at me, "No, Annie is with Andrea. As much as I would've loved to spend a morning with my daughter and husband, I figured that this should be an adults-only occasion. Where should we begin?"

She still sounds so measured, as if we aren't talking about one of the worst things I've ever done, probably the worst thing I've ever done. If she needs me to take the lead and show her the next steps I'm ready to take, then I can do that. I've done it at work before, and I can tackle this problem in the same way.

I step closer to her, but I stay on my side of the kitchen island. I can sense that physical proximity would not be welcome right now, but I want to be as close as she'll let me be.

"I love you, and I am so, so sorry that I did what I did last night. I-," I'm building up to lay out my plan to fix everything that I've done when Liv cuts me off.

"And exactly what did you do last night, Callum? You told me that you 'didn't go all the way,' but what does that mean to you?" She asks, taking another sip of tea before meeting my eyes again. God, I just want her to give me something, some sort of direction or indication as to what she's thinking or feeling. Liv has never iced me out like this before.

"We-do you think that's going to be helpful? Talking about the details right now?"

"I have no idea if it's going to be 'helpful' because I don't have a specific end goal in mind right now. I do know, however, that I deserve to know exactly what happened between my husband and the woman with whom he cheated. Tell me, Cal, and don't lie to me. I'll find out eventually."

She remains standing, but I drop myself into a bar stool, unbuttoning a few of the top buttons and rolling up my sleeves. I can't meet her eyes yet, and the small actions of settling buy me a moment or two. I won't be able to stall much longer, so I lay my forearms straight out on the table, palms up, and stare at the titanium band of my wedding ring against the dark granite of the counter.

"The pitch went well, and we all decided to celebrate. Emily said that she had a friend who owned a lounge and we should go there. We agreed to leave at 8, but I went to the hotel bar to write down my notes and things to follow up on. She joined me and bought us both a drink. I didn't ask for it; she just did it." I finally look up at Liv and see her staring at me. She's taken a few steps back to lean on the counter by the sink, still holding her tea.

Her grip on the mug is no longer relaxed but tense, as if she's using it to ground herself. However difficult this is for me, I know that it's infinitely worse for her, but she asked me to give her the truth, so I forge on.

"I only stayed about 5 minutes because I felt like she was being...weird, but I chalked it up to her being intense about her job. I went upstairs and called you. God, it feels like it was a year ago, but I was so happy to hear your voice. I told you about our plans, and-."

"I told you to be careful about Emily, and you brushed me off. Again."

"Yeah, I did. I need you to know that I did not go into the evening with any plans for something to happen. I don't think about her; I've never been tempted by her."

"That's a lie, Cal. I think that you believe it, but you don't cheat on your wife if you aren't tempted, and it's insulting for you to sit here and tell me that. Part of me asking for complete honesty is asking for you to be honest with yourself. You're attracted to her, you're around her all the time, and you allowed a relationship between the two of you to develop despite my express wishes."

I used to tell Liv that I wished I could see her in work mode, but if this is what it's like to be one of her clients, I'm glad that I never have. She's probably right about this, though, and I don't have anything to say to counter what she's telling me.

My head hangs, and I use the palms of my hands to rub at the irritation and ache behind my eyes.

"When we got off the phone, I wrote down a few more meeting notes and then got changed out of my suit before laying down. I met the group downstairs at 8, and we went to the lounge. It was all normal; Emily and I weren't even sitting next to each other." Deep breath, Cal. Get through this and show your wife the honesty that she deserves.

"We had a few rounds of drinks and shots before Jamie got up to dance, and the guys went to grab something to eat. Emily and I started talking about work, and then I decided that I needed to get up for a while."

"Why?" Liv speaks up from her perch against the counter.

"Why did I decide that I needed to get up? Well, I had a bit to drink and I needed to go to the bathroom, but looking back on it, I think that I wanted to get away from Emily. She started talking about men she worked with and then exes, and I just felt like it was maybe getting too personal. She was leaning closer to me, and I wanted to get away." Liv just nods silently at that, as if it's what she expected.

"I got up and told her that I needed the bathroom, and I guess she followed me. I didn't notice until I was in the hallway to the restroom, and she's on me, kissing me and pushing me up against the wall. Jesus, Liv, I hate having to tell you this," I pause here, but not for Liv. Reliving last night is making me feel like absolute scum because I can see all of the red flags.

In retrospect, I can see that Emily has been making attempts to get close to me for a while now. I can see how she thought that this trip would be the perfect time because I fed into that idea. I didn't tell her that I wasn't interested when, yeah, I can admit it now, I knew she had a bit of a crush. I had so many opportunities when I could have left last night, or joined Jamie or the others. I still don't 100% know why I gave in, but I wish that I had answers for the questions that I know my wife is going to ask.

"I kissed her back after a moment. I want so badly to tell you that I pushed her away, but I didn't. She started trying to ... touch me more, um, intimately, and that's when I realized what was happening. I called a car and went back to the hotel without everyone else. I sat down in my hotel room and called you. We talked, and then I slept for a few hours. Woke Jamie up early to tell her what happened so that she could be prepared if you needed anything. Changed my flight and made excuses so that I wouldn't have to see everyone. Came straight home."

Liv just nods again, and then looks down for a moment.

"Was she drinking as well?"

"Yeah, we had a drink at the hotel bar, and she was drinking pretty much the same as the rest of us, I think."

The silence stretches between us like an ocean. Deep, volatile, deceptively calm.

"Please say something, Liv."

"What do you want me to say? Do you want to hear, in detail, how that makes me feel? How I don't even feel like I'm in my actual body right now?" She sets her mug down and walks up to the island, leaning on her forearms. Her hands are only a few inches away from mine, her face close, and I can't break the eye contact that we have.

Her voice is lower now, "Or, should I tell you that all is forgiven because you're just so sad? Should I hug you and hold you while you cry to make you feel better? Please, Callum, please tell me what you need me to say to make this all better for you."

"I'll do anything. I've already looked at marriage counselors and an individual therapist. I'm prepared to quit my job tomorrow or transfer to a different department. Maybe I can figure out how to work from home and spend more time with Annie. I'll move out while we work on this and go at your pace. I don't care if it takes years, Liv. Anything you want."

I reach for her hands, but she pulls back, pushing off the counter and turning back to the sink to wash out her mug. I watch the elegant line of her neck, the graceful slope of her arms as she turns the water on and rinses the mug, turning it upside down on the dish rack.

"No," she says. "I don't want to do any of that. I don't want to work on us or take on counseling or have you quit your job. I've been trying to work on us for months, and you were simply not interested in listening to me, so I think that I'm done listening to you for a while.

"To be clear, we are no longer together, and I am going to file for divorce. For now, you'll go to our room and continue to pack your stuff and then move into the guest room. We'll tell Annie that we're just getting our own rooms, and we'll sound excited about it. We're going to convince her that we couldn't be happier to have separate rooms because when we have separate homes, we'll need to really sell it to her."

I'm stuck in the barstool, my voice not working while her volume builds.

"If Annie isn't around, you won't talk to me unless I talk to you first. You'll be honest with your parents that you ignored me for months and cheated on me the second you went out of town!" She yells. My wife never yells.

Somewhere after the word "divorce," I started to cry. I don't remember when exactly it started, but her figure is going blurry, and my throat is tight. I can see words in my head, but I can't get anything past the grief and humiliation and loathing bubbling inside me. I am mute in the face of my wife's disgust.

I had a plan, I had solutions, but she doesn't want any of them. All my wife wants is to leave me.

"And how dare you throw counseling and quitting at me like a consolation prize, like pity offers for your partner of ten years now that you've had your fun with someone else! Why should I have to do any of that? I'll be your wife, I'll raise your child, then I also need to forgive you and comfort you for months of neglect. No. I'm not going to do that for someone who would do this to me.

"You're still the same man you were when you cheated on me last night, Cal, and I don't want to look at you anymore. I don't want to hear what you think we need or what terms you're willing to grant now that there are actual consequences for your actions.

"You are such a goddamn cliche, Cal. Truly. The younger woman at work, the doting but insecure wife at home begging you for a scrap of attention, the illicit night on a business trip and then trying to come home and act like you still have a right to my time and emotional labor. It's boring, frankly, and I would have thought you more original."

She moves down the hallway and I wordlessly follow her, orbiting around her like a dying star. I think I might be dying, might be about to implode on myself. Maybe that's exactly what I did last night. Maybe I've already done that to myself and my wife, my daughter.

Each word cuts at me, flays me into little pieces at her feet. I can't say anything, can barely force air into my lungs as I look at her. I'm desperate to smell her, feel her pressed against me. I can see the years that we should have had ahead of us melting like a piece of plastic left on the stove. Acrid, poisonous, ugly.

She's at the front door, where she peeks out the window and then scoffs, an annoyed and disappointed sound.

"Move your fucking car. I'm going to Andrea's and you're going to have your stuff moved into the guest room by this evening," she says as she busies herself with her bag and keys. It seems like she truly cannot stand the sight of me because she doesn't even look up when I open the door and move my car out of her way.

I have to wipe my eyes a few times to be able to see clearly enough to maneuver out of the driveway, but it still feels like I have cotton balls stuck in them. One glance at the rearview mirror confirms that my eyes are red, swollen and puffy from travel, lack of sleep, and crying. I look like shit.

I'm still in my car when Liv backs out of the driveway heading in the direction of her sister's house; watching the street for a long time after I lose sight of her tail lights. I'm still in the car when I walk through the front door of our home, down the hallway to our bedroom, and see the organized and methodical way that Liv has started to remove me from her space. I'm still in the car when I continue that work for her, double checking that I got everything of mine out of the bathroom cabinets, the dresser, our closet, my nightstand.

I don't think that I'll ever get out of that car, watching my wife leave me. I don't think that I'll ever be able to leave the place where I was when it finally clicked that I had dealt a death blow to my marriage.

CHAPTER 13

Callum

The weeks following are a confusing mix of poignant, mundane, devastating, humiliating, and dissociating. Liv kept her word, and if I try to speak to her without her speaking to me first then she just walks out of the room. I tried to speak to her once, and she didn't so much as make eye contact with me before calmly striding out of the room. I didn't try again.

I took two days off when I got home, citing the trip and the stress leading up to it. In that time I ignored three calls from Emily to my work phone before I just powered it off. During those first few days, I watched Annie and Liv go about their lives, bearing witness to the routines and traditions that they've built without me. I don't know the oatmeal song that they've created, or the bathroom dance.

Watching my wife and daughter interact makes me feel like I'm watching a choreographed show; they move around and with each other unconsciously and I soak up the sight of them while I can. Annie knows exactly where Liv likes to kiss the top of her head and will present that spot for kisses when she can sense that Liv is going to lean down. Liv knows exactly what Annie's babble means, even though I can barely distinguish it as English. Everything about them presents a unit, a well-oiled machine. Meanwhile I'm just a man in the corner of the room, tagging along as they go about their day.

Seeing the confusion on Annie's face when I was home that first morning was simultaneously sweet and gut wrenching. Has my presence become such a novelty? I always felt like an incredible father because Annie would cling to me when I got home, but the more that I'm around the more that the novelty of "Dad" wears off. It becomes clear that her mother is the one Annie trusts to fulfill her needs. I'm good for a story or bath time, but not for the tears or the anger or the bruised knees. That all goes to Liv, the parent that Annie knows she can truly count on.

Liv is incredible at involving me with Annie, but I can see how much she wishes that she didn't have to. How she flinches when our hands accidentally brush each other's, how she'll take any opportunity to move away from me under the guise of giving Annie and I time together. But my wife is like the sun, and we are her moons. Annie seeks her out eventually, though I no longer have that right.

The first day that I'm home, after waking up in the guest room and feeling the weight of my actions upon me, I make a few swift decisions. I'll go in person to hand in my resignation, because I owe my boss that, at least. I'll hope that I've earned a good recommendation, because I'll probably be paying child support and alimony and I don't want Liv worrying about money.

I don't know that it'll make a difference for mine and Liv's marriage, but I can't ever let myself get to the place where I was before, ignoring my wife and the friends I trust, isolating myself and justifying that I was doing it all for them. I wasn't. I wanted that status of a promotion, I wanted the money and the security that would come with this deal. I wanted the ego boost of being admired. I wanted it all so bad that I blew up the rest of my life.

My next step is getting into therapy. Liv deserved for me to have done it a while ago, but I can at least do it now. She may be done with me but I make up my mind to become someone that she could love again. I hope that I can convince her to give me another chance in the future, but more than that, a man that Liv could love is a good man. I want to be that; for my wife, my child, my family, myself. I so desperately want to be good, to make the right decisions but I'm fucking up all the time. I find someone pretty quickly, and get the first available appointment I can.

Liv goes out the second day, after asking me if I could stay with Annie. I hate that she even has to ask, but I admit that I need her to give me a rundown of Annie's schedule. Have I been much more than a glorified babysitter to my own child? Surely a parent should be able to leave their child with the other parent and not have to tell them what to do. Yet again, it's a slap in the face for me to realize the toll that I have forced upon my wife.

I don't know how much longer I'll be allowed to stay here, so I spend our time together taking as many pictures of myself and Annie as I can. I'm nearly obsessive about documenting the home that Liv and I made, knowing that at any moment she would be right to ask me to leave. I scan copies of the family photos on the walls, take pictures of the height chart that we just started for Annie on the door to her bedroom, and I even take one of Liv's shirts. It's an impulsive choice, but one that I would make again. Just the smell of my wife is a small comfort and the knowledge that only a few days ago Liv's room was our room gives me vertigo.

Annie and I are reading a book on the couch when I'm struck with a memory from a few years ago, just one moment of the mundane toils of early parenthood. Liv and I were more exhausted than we'd ever been, and relied on each other as we paved our path as a new family of three with our screaming, perfect little baby. Liv and I would almost always get up with Annie together, maybe because we were both light sleepers at the time, but I think that we both needed the physical presence of the other person; the tangible reminder that we weren't in this alone. We would come out to the couch where Liv would feed Annie, and we had a little feed/clean station.

I would lean back against the couch and Liv would crawl between my legs, with her back to my front. Sometimes she would hold Annie, and sometimes she would be so exhausted that I would hold our baby to her breast and Liv would fall right back asleep. In the morning we would pass coffee or tea to each other and exchange sleepy smiles, knowing that we made a perfect little person together and that we were a team in keeping her alive and each other sane.

I'm not clear on how I got to this point, but I know that I was a good father once, a good husband. Liv's judgment is too good to have children with someone who didn't deserve her. I would race home to be with her, I would never make a decision without her. When did we stop being a team? When did I decide that I should make all of the decisions without my wife?

The questions bounce around every moment of every day; I can't escape them even when I get a few hours of fitful sleep on the lumpy mattress in the guest bedroom. I don't sleep much, but it feels like I'm seeing everything clearly for the first time in months, maybe longer.

When I can't sleep, I write everything down. The first time that the impulse grabs me, my pen shakes when it hits the paper. Not so long ago I was writing down my feelings about my wife, excited to start making things better. Now I'm writing down all of the ways that I made things worse.

I'm going to bring it all to my therapist to read because I'm not sure how much of this I can verbalize. Can I talk about my wife without choking up? Could I tell someone else about the way that we used to care for each other without my throat closing on me? Can I recall all of the moments where I ignored the most important person in my life without wanting to jump into traffic? I'm not sure, so I write it all down.

On the third day, I go into work, my resignation letter in my bag. The house is quiet when I wake, the girls still asleep. I don't need to bother making lunch for myself, but I walk into the kitchen anyway. I set out a mug and a tea bag for Liv next to the electric kettle that I fill. I cut up an apple for Annie and get out one of the almond butter packets that Liv will give her to snack on while she makes a real breakfast.

I tidy the few toys that Annie left out last night and fold a blanket over the back of the couch. These small acts of caring for my family open a dam inside, and before I know it I'm crying in the dark living room, crushed with the weight of knowing that my days here are numbered.

That's when Liv walks in, bleary and rumpled and soft from sleep. She's shuffling to the kitchen, hand already reaching for the kettle. She draws back for a moment when she realizes that there's water in it already, and then furrows her brow when she sees the mug and tea bag. She isn't used to me doing things like this anymore, even though they were a staple in our relationship previously.

I want to say something, anything, to make her see me. If for no other reason than to not frighten her. I don't want to speak, lest she walk out without getting her tea. Instead, I set my travel mug down on the coffee table. I wince when she gives a small jump, whirling around to see me in a full suit and tie, lingering in the dark living room like a ghost.

She takes a moment to study me before turning back to the kettle. She switches it on,placing both arms out to the sides, palms braced on the counter. Her back is tense, shoulders high.

"Going back to work?" She asks me. I want to fall to my knees at the chance that she's giving me to talk to her.

As it is, I have to clear my throat twice and take a drink of my coffee before I can get a decent work out.

"I should only be gone a few hours. I'm, um, handing in my resignation. I'll have health insurance through the end of the month and I'm already looking at a family plan for us if I can't find another job by then, so we should be covered. There's an apple in the fridge for Annie and if you want to go anywhere today I should be home by 11," I ramble.

She just nods, pouring water into her mug when it boils. She turns around and leans back against the counter, steeper her tea bag. This is nearly the same position that we were in when I first came home and the sense of deja vu is a special kind of horror, given our last conversation here.

"Why are you quitting?" She asks me.

I just blink for a moment, and then try to compress the 1000 reasons and words and explanations into a few sentences.

"Well," I say, "I can't work there anymore. I hate what I've done, and I think this job seemed to be the catalyst for me. I have a meeting with a therapist next week to talk about why and when I started to change, but this feels like the best first step to take. I can't go back and take back what I did -," Liv cuts me off here.

"You can't go back and take back cheating on me, you mean. I'd prefer it if you called it what it is, not just as "something you did". Be specific," she says, turning around to throw her tea bag in the garbage.

Her movements are confusingly nonchalant, as if we're talking about a grocery list and not me imploding our marriage.

I clear my throat again, "That's fair. I can't turn back time and stop myself from ... cheating on you," I have to fight the words out, "but I can avoid putting myself in that position again, with those same people."

"Quitting your job doesn't change anything for us, Cal. If you're trying to use this as a gesture, then it's not enough. There isn't one single thing that you could do, no gesture significant or grand enough to change my mind. We've been in the house together because of Annie, and because I deserve the extra help of you sometimes being around. So if you're doing this with the expectation that I'll fall at my feet and thank you for doing something for me, then allow me to correct that assumption now."

This is the first sign of emotion that I'm really seeing from Liv, and I bask in it. I hate that she hurts, I detest knowing that I caused it, but seeing her walk around so tightly controlled was awful. She's always prided herself on feeling her emotions and telling people how she feels, and I know how important that is to her. I will take her anger, her disappointment, her betrayal and hold them for her as long as I need to. At this point, I'll take anything that she wants to give me.

"You're right. I know there's nothing that I can do, and you've been more than fair about letting me stay here with you and Annie. I'm quitting because you were right about all of it, and me. I know that it isn't enough, and I don't have the answers right now for why I stopped listening to you. All I know is that I've become someone I'm not proud of and I need to change."

Liv grasps her mug in both hands, steeling herself for what comes next.

"When I wake up in the morning I have a few moments where I forget that you cheated on me. I still reach for you in the night. I look for you first thing. I have dreams about what our life used to look like, but I can't picture the future anymore. I used to have these visceral images of us with another baby, traveling with the kids, seeing them off to college. Ever since you called me to tell me that you cheated it's like I'm physically incapable of conjuring those visions again."

I would rather she have gutted me. Having to stand in a different room from my wife while she shows me her pain goes against every instinct that I have. I've changed, but I also have years of being her man instilled into me. My legs tense to move and I grip my travel mug to try to ground myself, but it doesn't work.

The next thing I know I'm rounding the kitchen island, going to my wife. We both set our mugs down on the counter with a 'thunk', carelessly spilling our drinks as we're pulled together like magnets. Her head knows to tuck into my neck and my hands run through her hair, one staying to cup her nape and hold her to me and the other arms bands around her shoulders. This might be the last time that I get to hold my Liv and the tears are back, for both of us. I let out an ugly, tortured sob against her hair and I can feel the scalding of her tears soaking my shirt.

We stay locked like that for a while; at this moment we aren't a couple on the verge of divorce, we're two people grieving a beautiful life that we would have had together. My grief is tinged with shame and I'm sure hers with betrayal but we grasp at the solace that we still find in this embrace. Trying to hold this in would be as futile as trying to pack sand into a colander.

Liv may no longer be able to picture our lives together, but I can see every moment. I can still see the other baby we should have had, I can see the trips and the holidays and the joy of watching our children grow up. I can see Liv grey and wrinkly, puttering about the beach house that I would have bought for her. I hope that I never lose those pictures, even though they'll only ever be a fantasy for me.

The flood of grief wanes eventually, and she pulls away. My arms instinctively tighten, not ready to let her go but I know that I need to. As soon as she moves away I reach behind me to the tissues on the kitchen windowsill and hand her a few, then grab some for myself.

"I know that there isn't a grand gesture to make up for the last few months, or for cheating on you. You're right about all of it, and I hate that I had to go this far and lose you to admit that. I know that I was a good man once, and I have to believe that I can be that again, as Annie's dad, but also as your friend and parenting partner. This is just the first step."

My work phone buzzes in the other room, and Liv looks at the clock on the stove, eyes as swollen and red as my own. The harsh red glow of the numbers hurts my dry eyes, but I can see that it's time for me to go. Even if I wasn't going to work this morning, Liv needs me gone.

"I'll be home around 11:00, I think. Can I text you if I'm going to be later than expected?" I ask her.

I'm going to be in the same building as the woman I cheated on my wife with so the least I owe her is a clear timeline of when I'll be home.

She just nods at me and I take my que to leave, giving her a wide berth as I go.

I'm on autopilot as I go into the office. I thought that it would feel surreal to know that I am making this drive for the last time, but it doesn't. As a matter of fact, I don't feel anything. After the emotional episode in the kitchen it's almost like I don't have anything left to give.

I park in my usual spot, noting that the lot is fuller than usual since I'm late this morning. I pull in a bit crooked, but it doesn't matter much. It's not like I'll be here long, anyway. I make a beeline for my boss's office, and I shut the door behind me when I see he isn't on a call. It's clear to him that something is going on, and his brows furrow.

"For someone who just crushed one of the biggest pitches we've ever had, you don't seem thrilled," he says.

I should enjoy the praise, but I still can't pull up any emotion, so I just nod.

"I need to hand in my resignation. I hate to do this to you, but I cannot work in this office anymore. I am happy to complete two more weeks of work, provided that I can work from home."

"Sit down," he says, gesturing to one of the leather chairs in the corner of his office. I follow orders, plopping down into it and resting my elbows on my knees.

"What happened between last week and now?" he asks me.

"I have let this job come between me and my family," I tell him, still hunched over my legs, "and I can't go on like this. I need to make a change and I can't do that while I'm tied to this job."

"Is it the job that you need to get away from or Emily?"

My head comes up then, the surprise of him knowing straightening my spine.

"Did she come to you?"

"No, but gossip about you two has been going on for a while and there's noise that something finally happened on this trip," he says, leaning back in his chair and crossing his hands over his lap.

"Yeah, something happened on the trip and Liv knows. Nothing happened before then, but it doesn't matter. I'm losing my family and I can't go on like this."

"Callum, we've known each other for a long time. I've known Liv for a long time, and I remember when Annie was born," he tells me. "That makes this so much worse, but I can't let you resign."

I start to open my mouth when I see him gesture someone in, and one of the HR reps steps into the office. I shut my mouth, unsure of where this is going.

"You may both be adults who consented to whatever happened, but she's young, new to this company, and you're her direct supervisor. We cannot tolerate relationships between supervisors and their direct reports, however brief they may be. From what you just told me, I don't have a choice but you terminate your employment contract with us, effective immediately."

The HR rep takes over at that point, outlining the next steps, my last paycheck, how to get a reference, when my healthcare coverage ends, and when I'll be locked out of my accounts. It's all just a buzz to me, an added humiliation that I deserve.

They save me the embarrassment of escorting me to my office, but I do have to immediately pack my things. While I'm gathering the few personal items that I kept in my office, I hear the door click shut. Expecting it to be Jamie, I look up and then freeze when I come eye-to-eye with Emily.

"Open the door," I tell her, but she just leans back against it.

"What's happening?" she asks, crossing one ankle over the other in what should look like a confident move, but instead it just looks like she can't stand still.

"I've been fired, Emily. Now open the door, you and I do not need to be having a closed door meeting."

"But we need to talk," she exclaims, pushing off the door and rounding to my desk.

I mirror her, grabbing the box of my effects and crossing to the door to open it.

"I think that it's best if you and I have no contact moving forward."

"If you don't work here anymore and your wife is leaving you then we can -."

"Who told you that my wife is leaving me?"

Her eyes turn shifty, "Considering what's been going on with us and then what happened I just thought that now we could try to really be together," she says.

I hate myself more in this moment. I wish that I could tell Liv, or myself, that this woman masterminded a grand plan to seduce me, but she didn't. She followed my lead, walked through the doors that I left open for her. She's an adult, and she bears some responsibility for what happened but it's clear that the bulk of it is on me. She has the idea that we could be together because I gave her that idea and then reinforced it every time I stayed late or ignored a call from my wife.

"Emily," I say gently, "I realize that I gave you the wrong impression, and for that I apologize, but it was never going to be you. There wasn't even a choice between you and my wife."

I watch her entire body just deflate, her mouth popping open.

"It was always going to be my wife, in the end. I can see that I used you for an ego boost, which wasn't fair to you. That being said, and I'm not trying to be cruel, but I know that you've gotten involved with coworkers in the past and I need you to be realistic. Being the other woman will never get you into a loving relationship, and he'll almost always stay with the woman he actually loves. Don't let this be a pattern for you."

And then I walk out, ignoring the looks of coworkers who certainly heard our conversation, or can at least piece together what was said and why I'm walking out of the office with my personal effects in a cardboard box. I blow out a huge breath when I get into the car, placing the box on the floor by the passenger seat. And then I start beating the steering wheel.

I hit it until my elbows ache with the impact and my knuckles are swollen, until the rage tamps down and I feel ready to drive. I don't know what the rest of my life will look like, this is the first thing that I've done in a while that feels right.